JANINE BEACHAM

LITTLE, BROWN BOOKS FOR YOUNG READERS
www.lbkids.co.uk

LITTLE, BROWN BOOKS FOR YOUNG READERS

First published in Great Britain in 2017 by Hodder and Stoughton

1 3 5 7 9 10 8 6 4 2

A CIP catalogue record for this book
is available from the British Library.

ISBN 978-1-51020-128-6

Printed and bound by CPI Group (UK) Ltd, Croydon, CR0 4YY

The paper and board used in this book are made
from wood from responsible sources.

Little, Brown Books for Young Readers
An imprint of Hachette Children's Group
Part of Hodder and Stoughton
Carmelite House
50 Victoria Embankment
London EC4Y 0DZ

An Hachette UK Company
www.hachette.co.uk

www.hachettechildrens.co.uk

To my family

Prologue

Watchful the cat leapt frantically from rooftop to rooftop. He slithered on to a window ledge, righted himself, and sprang to the cobblestones. A carriage rattled past, and Watchful whisked his tail away just in time. He raced to the back door of a mansion, and meowed until the door opened. A butler smiled down at him.

'Hungry, old thing? Here you are – a nice bowl of cream.'

The cat ignored it, swishing his tail. Surprised, the butler stroked his head.

'What's the matter? Been chased by a dog?'

Watchful yowled.

'Fussy this morning, eh?' said the butler. 'Well, I must serve breakfast to the master. If you wait like a good kitty, you can have the kipper bones.'

Just as he lifted his tray, he heard a knock at the back door.

'Bother,' said the butler.

The cat ran in front of him and nipped his ankle.

'Hey!' said the butler, offended. 'You nearly tripped me! Out of the way, for goodness' sake.' He picked up the wriggling, protesting cat, and shut him in the pantry. 'Sorry,' he whispered.

Then he went to open the door. Watchful scratched and hissed, knocking over tins and canisters.

The butler saw the face of his visitor.

But did not see the sword blade until it entered his chest.

Chapter 1

Murder at the Breakfast Table

'Dear me,' said Lady Constance Raventhorpe, lowering the newspaper. 'Another butler murdered. How very uncivilised.'

Her daughter Rose dropped her toast. 'Did you say murder, Mother?'

'Oh, it's not as if it's anyone we know,' said her mother, bored. 'My goodness, the climate of Yorke kills off people all the time. Look at all those sickly governesses.'

Rose glanced anxiously at their own butler. He

sliced the top off a boiled egg with mathematical precision. 'Another cup of tea, madam?'

'Yes, thank you, Argyle,' said Her Ladyship. 'And perhaps another egg.'

'How can you say that, Mother? It's horrible!' cried Rose.

'I agree. The eggs are decidedly under par,' said Lady Constance. 'Argyle, tell Mrs Standish to boil them half a minute longer.'

'I meant the murder,' Rose said. 'Pass me the newspaper.'

'Pass me the newspaper, *please*,' her mother corrected. 'Or better still, ask Argyle to do it.'

Argyle gave a wry smile and resumed arranging the bowl of eggs.

Rose stared down at her plate. She took a deep breath. 'Please.'

Argyle went to the sideboard and lifted a new, perfectly pressed newspaper, smoothing it carefully before placing it to the side of Rose's plate. He swept crumbs from the tablecloth with a brush and pan, and poured more tea for Lady Constance. Then he added milk, and stirred the tea with a delicate silver spoon.

'My hand mirror, please,' ordered Lady Constance.

Rose repressed a sigh as Argyle fetched the item from the sideboard. Lady Constance held it up to admire her flawless complexion, chestnut tresses and slender neck. Rose, whose pointed chin, freckles and ordinary hazel eyes were the despair of her mother, did her best to ignore this. Quickly she turned the pages of the newspaper. She noted an article about her father, Lord Frederick, the Baron of Yorkesborough:

Our Ambassador to the Crown, Lord Frederick Raventhorpe of the ancient Yorke family, continues his fight against the opium trade. 'I know this is a sticky matter in our nation, where a great deal of cash is made on the stuff,' His Lordship stated. 'However, I have learned

about the nasty effect of this drug in the Far East, and I am dashed if I will allow it to go on. Shameful business in all respects.'

Rose smiled. Father had been remarkably polite in the newspaper. At home, he ranted at length about the corruption of people in high places, and their cruel abuse of underlings. She had learned some impressive Arabic swearwords from him.

Then she found the article about the murders.

SILVER SERVICE STABBING, screamed the headline. WAS IT FOR THE CUTLERY?

The victim was the second butler to be stabbed in a week. ('Second!' whispered Rose. 'Did the newspaper not even bother to report the first one? I bet it was because he was a servant.') Both had been killed on their employers' doorsteps. A black glove had been left at each scene. The police believed the attacks – now called the Black Glove murders – were botched burglaries. Inquiries were continuing.

'Now Rose,' said her mother, raising an eyebrow. 'Do not get worked up. Newspapers always exaggerate.'

Argyle presented a napkin on a tray. Lady Constance patted her lips. 'I shall be going out this morning to have my portrait painted. If you go for a walk, Rose, I expect you to be back in time for tonight's party.'

'Oh,' said Rose. 'That.'

'I've completed the menu,' her mother continued, giving her a list. 'As you requested, I am keeping it simple.'

Pour l'anniversaire de Rose

Potage à la Raventhorpe
Parsnip and truffle soup

Sole à la Raventhorpe
Sole fillets baked with horseradish cream

Pigeonneau Raventhorpe
Pigeons poached in Raventhorpe champagne

Mousse à la Raventhorpe
Mousse of quail from the Raventhorpe estate

Rôti de chevreuil Raventhorpe
Roast venison with truffle sauce and potatoes Dauphinoise

Sorbet à l'abricot Raventhorpe
Apricot sorbet with brandy cream and toffee baskets

Soufflé à la fleur d'orange
Orange-flower soufflé

Meringues à l'eau de rose avec crème chantilly
Rose-water-flavoured meringues with cream

Gâteau napolitain
Twelve-layered birthday cake on three tiers with icing roses

Fromages
A selection of thirty cheeses from France

Coffee and fine wines

'Ah,' said Rose. 'Yes. Very simple!'

'Only fifty guests or so,' agreed her mother. 'But they are all important. So no showing off with silly languages.'

'Mother, I wouldn't—'

'I was mortified at how you behaved to your cousin last year. Mortified! Talking in Arabic. What on earth possessed you?'

'Marjorie was being rude to Argyle, Mother. I only called her a daughter of a snake. I know it wasn't polite, but she didn't understand a word—'

'Rose.'

Argyle busily folded napkins into fans. Rose looked at the tablecloth. 'I'm sorry, Mother.' *Na'am*, she added in her mind. *Yes, Mother.*

'Your father will be home tonight for the party.' Lady Constance dropped a kiss on her daughter's head. 'Happy twelfth birthday, Rose.'

'Thank you,' said Rose. She swallowed, knowing that was as much affection as she'd receive from her mother, even on her birthday.

Lady Constance finished her tea and rose to her feet. The embroidered tulle of her peach silk gown swirled around her. Silver beads glittered on her bodice.

Rose waited, holding her breath.

With a stately rustle, and trailing of lily-of-the-valley perfume, Her Ladyship left the room.

When the door closed behind her, Rose turned around so fast her plait whipped her shoulder.

'Argyle! Did you hear about this?' She stabbed

a finger at the newspaper. 'Murdered butlers! Did you know the victims?'

Argyle replaced the devilled kidneys in their dish, and frowned.

'I can't say for sure, lass. But it's troubling. I never heard the like of it.'

Rose rested her chin in her hand. 'I don't believe it's a botched burglary. Wouldn't most burglars break in through a window at dead of night? They'd hardly knock at the door and wait for the butler to answer.'

Argyle picked up the paper and pointed to a line. 'It says the latest murder was in Vicarsgate. Let me see, who do I know in Vicarsgate?'

Rose knew that street. She and Argyle had spent many happy hours exploring Yorke's medieval walls and twisted, ancient thoroughfares. It was astonishing to think of murder happening in quiet, respectable Vicarsgate.

Ordinarily Rose would have loved to hear more, but she was too worried to be amused.

'Several families,' mused Argyle. 'Including the Bagtree sisters. Twins. They live at opposite ends of their mansion. The ladies never agree, so they have two butlers. The old fellows spend all day passing messages between them. "Tell Miss Serena Bagtree she is an old bat." "Inform Miss Eleanor Bagtree that she is a hollow-toothed viper." They only see each other at church and at Christmas. Then they fight over dinner while the butlers decorate each sister's Christmas tree.'

'Just don't answer the door to strangers,' she ordered Argyle.

'I can hardly help doing that, lass,' said Argyle drily, placing the newspaper back on the table. 'It is my duty as a butler.'

'But what if it's the murderer at the door?'

'Oh, no murderer would bother with the likes of me.' Argyle rearranged the flowers on the table and inspected a candlestick for dust. He seemed completely unconcerned.

Rose frowned. 'All the same . . . I shall talk to Father about it.'

She drank some tea, and felt calmer. As long as Argyle was around she could not panic. Argyle feared nothing.

'Now, before you leave—' Argyle cleared his throat. 'I don't go in for fuss. But I thought you should have a wee token for your birthday.'

He held out a small box. Rose opened it. Nestled in velvet was a cameo necklace, carved to depict a black cat. Rose opened a catch to reveal a small space behind the carving. A locket.

'Oh, Argyle,' breathed Rose. 'It's perfect. Absolutely perfect!'

'Aye, well,' said Argyle, coughing again. 'Just a small remembrance of the—'

There was a knock at the front door.

Rose's smile faltered. Argyle glanced at her, then back towards the door.

Another knock.

Rose stared at him. 'Argyle, don't . . . '

The butler set his jaw. He stalked into the hallway and opened the door. Rose heard voices. Murderers? She pushed back her chair and ran out into the hall. A black-clad figure loomed on the threshold.

'Happy birthday!' squealed Emily Proops.

Rose sagged against the wall in relief.

Emily Proops always wore mourning from top to toe. This was in memory of her late Pomeranian dog. She was a tall girl of fifteen, older than Rose, but Rose preferred her as a friend to most of the girls in Yorke.

'Are you coming for a walk, Rose? It's a perfect day for it. I have a new black parasol, and I'm dying to show it off.'

Argyle held the door open wider, and smiled at Rose. Beyond Emily, she could see the sunny blue skies of the city, and the skyline with its towering cathedral. The whole city was embraced by ancient grey stone walls, built in ancient times to protect it against attack. 'Enjoy yourself, lass.'

Rose beamed back. Then she put on her favourite hat – crammed with pink and cream roses and topped by an ostrich feather – and went out with Emily into the sparkling sunshine of Yorke.

Chapter 2

The Ravensgate Cat

'I want to see the cats.'

Emily groaned. 'Rose! Must you?'

'It's my birthday,' said Rose. 'You have to indulge me.'

Yorke's cat statues were scattered all over the city. They could be spotted on streets from Barleygate to Tatterlace Green. Yorke's streets were called 'gates', based on names from Viking days. The statues sat on walls, roofs and windowsills. Rose's favourite was the Groatsgate statue. That cat was reading a book.

Visiting them all took the best part of a morning. They passed pedlars, housewives with baskets, flower-sellers and delivery boys. Autumn was on its way, and the tree leaves were turning scarlet. Despite the unpleasant news of the morning, Rose's spirits soared. This walk was as close to freedom as she could get.

Emily sighed, tucking blonde curls under her hat. 'Why do you like the cats so much?'

'Because Argyle has taken me on walks to see them, ever since I was little. Mother and Father were too busy to take me out much. The funny thing about the cats is that nobody knows much about them. But Argyle said there is a prophecy.' She recited:

While all the Cats of Yorke keep watch
On enemy and foe
The city is protected
By the Guardians below.
But if the cats are taken

Then the Guardians will fall
The dead will rise up from their graves
And ruin will come to all.

'The dead will rise?' repeated Emily. A passing woman shot her a horrified glance. Emily smiled sweetly in return.

'It's an ancient superstition. If the cats disappear, the city will be cursed.'

'Ugh. How wonderfully horrible!'

That reminded Rose. 'Did you hear about those poor butlers being stabbed? I wondered if your butler had said anything.'

'Spillwell?' Emily sniggered. 'All he ever says is "very good, madam". Father suggested he carry a pistol, but Spillwell said it would only be one more thing to polish.'

They crisscrossed the streets, visiting cat after cat. Yorke's great walls, circling the city, loomed over the rooftops. The streets bustled. 'Lovely day,' the gentlefolk said to them. Shop-owners called out their wares. 'A ribbon for tha' hair, miss!' 'A watch-chain for your beau?'

The girls crossed the green surrounding the cathedral. The great Cathedral of Yorke Minster was the city's pride. Its bells could be heard out on the moors. Every inch of carved stone was a work of art, and its stained glass windows were masterpieces. Its very dust carried the weight of centuries.

'I grant you the cat statues are important to Yorke,' said Emily. 'But I prefer the gargoyles on the cathedral roof and the sarcophagi in the crypt – there's nothing like a good tomb.'

Rose laughed. 'There's nothing like your Gothic taste, Emily.'

They came to Argyle's favourite cat statue, on a ledge on Ravensgate.

'Argyle said this cat is the oldest in Yorke,' said Rose, as they approached. 'There's a story that on moonlit nights it sits on top of that gas lamp.'

'Oooh,' said Emily happily. 'The perfect subject for a tragic poem.'

Rose looked up, expecting the familiar sight of the cat watching for birds. Sunlight filled her eyes, making her squint. She tilted her hat. The gas lamp was there, of course. The ledge was still the same. High above the street, providing the statue with an excellent view of the long street of Ravensgate.

A strange, cold sensation filled Rose's stomach.

The statue was missing.

There was nothing to suggest why it was gone. No sign, no chipped paint, nothing.

'Well, that's . . . funny,' said Emily. She glanced quickly at her friend. 'I'm sure it's nothing to worry about,' she added, unconvincingly. 'Perhaps it's being cleaned. Or repaired.'

'But they've never disappeared,' said Rose faintly. 'Never!'

The prophecy. *The dead will rise up from their graves* . . . She spun around as if an army of ghosts was marching towards her. Only the usual uncaring crowds walked by. Why had the statue disappeared? Why now, on her birthday of all days?

Emily patted her arm. 'It's nothing, I'm sure. I mean, it can't have anything to do with that prophecy. I don't see the dead rising up from anywhere!' She attempted a laugh. 'Well, I don't think they would. It's only one statue, after all.'

'But . . . ' said Rose. She wanted to argue. It would be very difficult to get up to that ledge, even with a ladder. Why had someone gone to such trouble to steal a statue?

Suddenly she turned on her heel. Emily hurried in her wake, so quickly her jet-black petticoats swished above her ankles.

Rose pushed through the crowds. She heard indignant exclamations, an 'ow' or two, and a sniffy 'Well! How uncouth!'

'Pardon me,' Rose stammered, trying to keep track of her whereabouts.

Two more cat statues were missing. Rose's

legs felt unsteady. It was like seeing the cathedral disappear, or the ancient city walls razed.

'I suppose you're right,' she heard herself say. 'They are being cleaned. That's the logical explanation.'

Emily fidgeted with the black ribbons on her hat. 'Rose, I'm sorry, but it's nearly ten. Can't we go to the park now?'

Rose started out of her reverie. 'Of course,' she said. 'You've been so patient. Let's go.'

In the distance, children were singing a skipping rhyme.

Here come the Crowmen
up ahead.
Don't let them catch you
out of bed.
They like the darkness,
not the sun.
If you should see them,
run, run, run.

Rose shivered again. The skyline of Yorke was as beautiful as ever, but she could only think of those spaces where the cat statues had been.

Emily's chatter didn't cheer Rose up, but when they returned to Rose's door in Lambsgate she presented Rose with a birthday gift – a book of Gothic poetry, titled *The Darkness of My Imprisoned Soul, Volume XIV.*

Rose had barely thanked her and waved goodbye when Lady Constance swept her daughter upstairs. 'One must be suitably attired for one's guests, Rose,' she insisted. Agnes the maid helped Rose out of her clothes. Then Agnes beat egg yolks, rubbed them into Rose's hair, and rinsed them out with rose water and brandy. Dresses were tried on, presents put on display, and the house filled with flowers. Rose, under the onslaught of curling-irons and petticoats, had no chance to talk to Argyle.

By six o'clock, Lady Constance was rustling about in crimson brocade and calling for the Raventhorpe diamonds. Clad in her best dressing-gown, Rose watched this important process. Argyle was in charge of opening the safe and presenting Lady Constance with the velvet-lined boxes. Lady Constance's maid fastened the bracelet on Her Ladyship's wrist, and secured the tiara in her mistress's hair. Rose then watched her mother inspect the dining room, which sparkled with silver and crystal.

Argyle drilled the servants with last-minute instructions. It was his role to announce the guests, and assist in serving the dinner. Lord Frederick Raventhorpe arrived from the House of Lords, and gave Rose a birthday hug. Broad-shouldered and booming of voice, he had a flourishing moustache and a forehead sunburnt from travelling. 'Grand evening we're going to have!' he assured her. 'A real grown-up party for my girl. Twelve years old! I'll make sure old Argyle gets everything organised. Now off you go.'

Rose hurried upstairs.

Agnes helped Rose get ready. Her dress was a

lustrous pearl colour, its skirt so full and ruffled she had to gather it up with a great swoosh before she sat down. The bodice was hand-embroidered and the dainty capped sleeves were of Valenciennes lace. Cream rosebuds were tucked into Rose's hair. Then Agnes returned downstairs, and Rose waited alone for her grand entrance.

She was fiddling nervously with her sleeves when she saw Argyle in the doorway. He clapped a hand to his forehead, and pretended to reel with admiration.

'Don't be silly, Argyle.' Rose blushed.

'You look like a grown-up young lady,' said Argyle. 'Too grown-up, in fact, to need a butler looking after you.'

'Don't say that,' Rose protested. 'I couldn't do without you.'

Argyle shook his head. 'Your father needs help in the Far East. I'm thinking I should go out there soon, and help him.'

'Oh,' said Rose, dismayed.

'It's important work he's doing.' Argyle cleared his throat. 'I had a younger brother once. Wanted to be a Byronic poet. Thought ruin would make him a genius. He drank too much, took opium, and died when he was twenty.'

Argyle rarely spoke about his past. 'I didn't know,' Rose said. 'That's very sad. If – if you do go with Father, will you come back?'

'Of course, lass,' Argyle promised. 'Now it's high time you made your appearance. You go on downstairs.'

'Wait,' said Rose. 'I have to tell you something.'

'Now?' Argyle frowned. 'Lass, this is hardly the time for chitchat.'

'But it's important! Argyle, three of the cat statues have gone missing. Even your favourite on Ravensgate.'

To her horror Argyle turned ashen, staggering against the wall. Rose seized his arm.

'Argyle! I'm sorry! I'll get you some brandy.'

'No!' With a great effort, he straightened up. 'There,' he said, breathing hard. He wiped his face with a handkerchief. 'Right as rain.'

Rose was shaken. 'You need a doctor.'

'No I don't, lass!' His eyes flashed.

'But—'

'Go on downstairs.'

'I'm sorry,' said Rose. 'I'm sorry I mentioned it.' She felt wretched. But how could she have known it would upset him that badly? Was it because of the prophecy?

'There now, it's nothing. Go and join your guests.'

Reluctantly, Rose started downstairs. Her face burned with guilt. She should never have mentioned the statues. But they had always been special to Argyle, and to Rose too. He had given her the cat cameo specially . . .

She stopped in dismay.

'My cameo! I forgot to put it on.'

Argyle paused on the stair behind her.

'It can wait, lass. Her Ladyship—'

'I won't go in without it. I'll get it. You go down and announce me.'

Picking up her skirts, she ran back to her room.

Now, what had she done with it?

She turned up the lamps, illuminating the green and gold wallpaper. The cameo wasn't in her jewellery box or on her canopied bed, or among the velvet cushions on the window seat. It wasn't on her piano, and Rose didn't remember putting it on her dressing-table. She searched the collection of foreign souvenirs on the mantelpiece, followed by the sofa, the bookcase full of dictionaries, and the antique carpet Lord Frederick had rescued from a derelict château in the Loire.

As a last resort she looked under the bed. She shoved the blankets and quilts out of the way, peering underneath. Oh, there was that miniature portrait of Great-aunt Isolda! The maids always said the painted likeness scowled at them. But they would get in terrible trouble if Lady Constance found it here, so Rose snagged it out and put Great-aunt Isolda safely away in a drawer.

She returned to her search. It took a minute's awkward wriggling and stretching before she found the cameo. Then she straightened up, put the chain around her neck and dusted down her crumpled dress.

Finally, she left her room for the stairs. Resting her hand on the banister, she composed herself, and started down the steps.

A draught riffled her skirts. She hesitated, wondering if late guests had arrived. If so, she should wait for Argyle to announce them.

The breeze – a definite breeze now – raised goosebumps on her skin. A door slammed, making her jump violently.

Then came the crash.

Rose leapt downstairs. Her skirts tripped her.

Ruffles tore. She came to a skidding halt in the entrance hall.

Argyle lay sprawled on the floor. Blood trickled over the marble. His eyes were wide and shocked, unseeing. In his hand he clutched a single black glove.

Chapter 3

Swords in the Cemetery

It had been several days since the funeral. Rose stood alone in the graveyard.

The evening sky glowed pink and grey, casting the River Knoll with a silver hue. She could hear horses' hooves trotting in distant streets. Here, the tombstones lay veiled in ivy, or carpeted with moss and rotting leaves. Tree branches had grown into fantastical shapes, resembling scrawled, indecipherable letters. The gales from the moors treated trees as mere playthings.

Rain began to patter on the gravestones. Rose did not move. A soaking was the least she deserved. Memories flashed through her mind – someone pulling her away from the body – a sobbing maid scrubbing blood off the floor – shocked guests – police asking questions. Lord Frederick and a couple of the hardier guests had run outside to see if they could spot the murderer, but the street had been deserted.

'He was after my diamonds, I'm sure,' Lady Constance had told the police.

The next morning, she had fought a pitched battle with Rose over her desire to wear mourning. Rose had got up, heavy-eyed from a sleepless night, and asked Agnes to help her into her one black dress. Her mother had taken one look at her and gasped in horror.

'I will not have you looking like Emily Proops. In mourning for her Pomeranian! Whatever next?'

'Mother, I cared about Argyle.' Rose was exhausted. Had she really expected her mother to understand? 'He was kind, and clever, and fun, and—'

An expression of distaste crossed Lady Constance's features. 'Rose Raventhorpe! I have told you time and again that this attachment will not do. Young ladies do not wear mourning for servants. We shall pay for his funeral, and that will be more than adequate.'

Rose had finally compromised with a purple and black striped dress. The only jewellery she wore was her cameo.

So the funeral had been held. But Rose missed Argyle so badly she had returned to the gravesite.

The headstone was in place, with its freshly cut epitaph. Rose had insisted on its wording, and her parents had given way. Lord Frederick had been fond of the butler.

ARGYLE

Devoted Friend

and

Butler of Quality

But there was something new, and extremely strange. A contraption had been fitted over the grave – a flat, ugly cage of iron bars. Rose stared at the thing, and tried to work out its purpose. Surely it was not a decoration. Who had put it there, and why?

Footsteps crunched on the path. Rose closed her eyes and willed the intruder away.

The footsteps came closer. They stopped at the grave.

Rose opened her eyes. A great black umbrella opened over them both. Its owner was a man.

The man's face was weathered and strong, his hair salted with grey, and his blue eyes compelling. He wore a long coat over striped trousers, and black shoes. He smelled of silver polish and tea.

He cleared his throat.

'I am very sorry, Miss Raventhorpe.'

Rose scrubbed the tears from her face with a handkerchief.

'Thank you,' she said, in a muffled voice. 'Were you acquainted with Argyle, sir?'

'Yes,' said the man. 'He was a friend.'

Rose peered at him.

'I didn't see you at the funeral.'

'No. It was ... unwise in the circumstances. I am sorry I missed it.'

'It was a noble send-off,' said Rose. 'We had a piper play the bagpipes, and I read some of the poetry of Robert Burns.'

The man smiled. 'He would have liked that. Be assured, Miss Raventhorpe, when we have the chance, I and his other friends will bid him farewell properly.'

Other friends? Rose was bewildered. What other friends? Hadn't Argyle devoted his life to her?

She looked at the man again, his pinstriped trousers and smart coat. *Oh. Of course.* 'You're a butler?' she asked. 'Whose family do you serve?'

'I am head butler at a respectable establishment

in Yorke.' He bent to touch the iron bars surrounding Argyle's grave. 'I am so sorry you had to witness his death. It must have been terrible.'

'Yes,' said Rose. She tried to push the memories away. 'Wouldn't I know the family you work for?' she prodded.

'Oh, I don't think it likely,' said the butler. He paused. 'No doubt this will get into the papers. The third Black Glove murder.'

'I want to find out who killed him,' said Rose. She added, fiercely, 'I *must* find out.'

'So must I,' said the butler grimly. 'And discover who is stealing the cat statues.'

Rose gaped. 'You know about them?'

'We all do,' said the man, as if that was a satisfactory answer. He looked thoughtfully for a moment at Rose's cameo. Then he indicated the iron contraption. 'Now, no doubt you are wondering about this mortsafe. I ordered it to be placed here. I apologise for the presumption, but it is an unfortunate necessity. You see—'

Somewhere nearby a twig snapped. The butler whirled around with the speed of a panther. It was astonishing behaviour for a man whose proper role was carrying trays and serving crumpets.

There was a yowl, and a bedraggled cat wriggled through the graveyard gates. The butler watched the creature as it searched for cover from the rainstorm, his shoulders visibly relaxing beneath the dark wool of his butler's coat.

'You should not be here, Miss Raventhorpe,' he said, turning back to her. Rose suddenly saw how tired he looked. 'It is loyal of you, and Argyle would be proud. But it is not safe.' The corner of his eye twitched as he gave a quick scan of the grounds.

Rose opened her mouth to argue. Surely he was being overcautious. Who would pose a threat here?

Then she paused. Three people had stepped through the cemetery gates.

One was a sullen-faced boy not much older than

Rose herself. The second was a slouching weed of a man, carrying a spade. The third was a pretty woman, whose fair hair shone beneath a velvet hat.

Gently, the butler pushed Rose behind a stone monument. Rose wanted to stand her ground – she was a Raventhorpe, after all – but the look in the butler's steely eye changed her mind. She pressed her body against the side of the monument and peered round.

As the strangers approached, she saw that the woman's hat was faded with wear, and there were holes in her handsome dress. Her eyes were wide, and had a calculating look.

'Heddsworth! What a delightful surprise,' she said.

'Miss Deacon,' said the butler. He conveyed disdain as delicately as a queen would sneeze into a handkerchief.

Miss Deacon sighed. 'We came to pay our respects to Argyle. Poor man. Such a tragedy.'

'If you wish to honour him, I suggest you leave him in peace.'

The slouching man kicked the iron contraption on Argyle's grave. 'Your doing, eh?' he sneered.

'Naturally, Blackthorn,' said Heddsworth. 'I am not prepared to see my friend's body dug up for sale, and dismembered.'

'Dear me,' Miss Deacon purred. 'You misunderstand us. We wish nothing but honour for Argyle.'

'Then you should get out of here – now!' Heddsworth's eyes glinted with fury.

The slouchy man – Blackthorn – sniffed insolently. Strolling over to a gnarled old apple tree, he scooped up one of the fallen fruit. He started tossing it in his hand. 'We just want to plant some flowers, is all.' He threw the apple higher. 'How about you show us some respect?'

Heddsworth's umbrella fell to the ground, its handle looking curiously hollow. A silvery blade flashed out, glinting in the pale evening light.

Swish.

The apple fell to the ground, sliced in half.

Heddsworth had drawn a rapier.

Rose almost forgot to breathe.

A butler with a sword?

'I see we are not welcome,' Miss Deacon said, looking amused. 'We shall have to visit another time. Come on, boys.'

Blackthorn grunted, and settled his spade over his shoulder. The sullen boy stared in Rose's direction. She ducked back behind the monument, heart thudding.

'Mortloyd,' the woman said sharply.

With a last malevolent look, the boy turned away. Miss Deacon led her strange company out of the graveyard.

Rose straightened her shoulders and emerged.

'Mr Heddsworth,' she said. 'Why are you carrying a sword?'

Heddsworth picked up his umbrella and replaced the rapier in its handle.

'Oh, I find it comes in useful,' was his reply. 'A pistol is convenient, but I prefer a rapier. Of course, one cannot always carry an umbrella for easy concealment, so a walking stick comes in handy.'

Rose began to wonder if Heddsworth was a butler at all. He couldn't have known Argyle. Argyle would definitely have mentioned a sword-wielding butler friend. The other unpleasant thought was that Argyle had been stabbed to death by someone wielding a sword . . . Rose moved a careful distance from Heddsworth.

'Why did you threaten those people? Who were they?'

'They are the Crows,' said Heddsworth. 'Grave-robbers. The reason for the mortsafe contraption.'

'Grave-robbers?'

Rose felt nauseous. That people would dig up Argyle's body – or anybody's loved one – to sell to doctors for dissection! Was it not enough that Argyle had been murdered?

'Is that why you have a sword? To protect yourself in this graveyard?'

Heddsworth shook his head. 'Not entirely, Miss Raventhorpe. I've carried one for a very long time.'

'But you're a butler!'

Heddsworth glanced up at the twilight sky, the rising moon. Fog thickened in the graveyard. A lonely crow cawed from a tree.

Heddsworth took on a businesslike manner.

'It's too late for you to be out alone, Miss Raventhorpe. Have you a carriage?'

'No, I walked. It wasn't far from home. But I want to know—'

'Walked? By yourself? I shall have to order a hansom cab to take you back. Really, Miss Raventhorpe, you should know better! Her Ladyship will be most upset.'

'She doesn't know,' said Rose stubbornly. 'She's entertaining guests. I left by the servants' door. I had to pay my respects to Argyle.'

The butler sighed, and looked at her more kindly. 'You are a brave child, but you have seen what kind of people prowl about here.'

Rose swallowed hard.

'I did see. Will they come back? Will that mortsafe thing be enough to protect the grave?'

'He will be protected,' said Heddsworth. 'I will remain here tonight.'

Rose stared at him, incredulous. 'Alone? All night? But there's the mortsafe—'

'Come along, Miss Raventhorpe.'

He led her out of the graveyard gates and hailed a hansom cab. The horse's hooves rang on the cobblestones, and the cab loomed out of the fog in a ghostly manner. Rose shivered in the seeping cold.

Heddsworth helped Rose into the vehicle, and Rose gave the driver her address. The man flicked his whip, and the vehicle rolled off.

Rose stared out of the carriage window. With a jolt, she realised that she still didn't know where

Heddsworth worked. How on earth would she find him again?

The last thing she saw before the fog obscured her view was a tall figure, returning to stand vigil at the grave.

Chapter 4

The Shudders

Of all the streets in Yorke, Rose most loved the Shudders.

The name had once been 'Shutters'. This came from the cobbled alley being so narrow that the window shutters of opposite buildings almost touched in the middle. It retained a medieval air, with houses that had already been old in the days of the Tudors. The Shudders had Rose's favourite haunts: Glyph and Brackett's bookshop, and

Dorabella's teashop, with its famous Yorke buns and gingerbread cats. Rose usually lingered over the dainties in Dorabella's windows . . . but today she walked purposefully past them.

My name is Rose Raventhorpe. Last week someone murdered my butler. He was my best friend and my champion. I am a Raventhorpe, and this city is under my family's protection. I will see justice done.

She passed Dr Jankers' medical school. A sign advertised 'Purveyor of Necrodrops: best cure for the Dreadful Difficulties of Sleeplessness.' The shop staff were setting up for the day, arranging goods in tempting displays. Rose sidestepped a bucket of soap suds and entered Fordingham Drapers. The shopkeeper bustled over.

'Would you like to see our handkerchiefs, miss? Lovely embroidery, just in from Paris.'

'Not today, thank you. I was wondering – do you sell gloves?'

The draper blinked in surprise. 'Why yes, we

do. Most folk go to Hall and Gantry's,' he said. 'Down the street. Claim to have the best selection in Yorke. But,' he added quickly, 'our gloves are most superior. If miss requires gentlemen's gloves, we have—'

'Black gloves?' broke in Rose. 'Formal gloves, like butlers', but black.'

'Black gloves, miss? Butlers don't wear—'

'But if they wanted to?'

'Well,' said the man, his smile fixed. 'No. Not that sort. Satin for ladies, leather for riding, and kid gloves. If miss would like a pair—'

'Thank you, but no. Another time.'

'Very good, miss.'

She made her way to Hall and Gantry's. A bell tinkled as she entered. She smelled fine leather, thick tweed and shaving cream. The shopkeeper, bent with age, looked up from a ledger. 'May I be of assistance, miss?'

'I understand you have the finest selection of gloves in Yorke,' said Rose.

'How very kind, miss! Ours are indeed first class gloves. Best you can buy. In fact,' he added proudly, 'we're the chosen supplier of Silvercrest Hall.'

'Silvercrest Hall?'

'The butlers' academy, miss! Everyone in society relies on Silvercrest Hall butlers.'

'Oh.' Rose struggled to hide her astonishment. 'Is it in Yorke?'

'Yes indeed. Number one hundred and one, Ravensgate.'

Rose made a mental note of the address. 'And do you sell black gloves?' she continued.

'Is it for a bereavement? Mourning dress?'

'Something like that.'

'We have just the thing.' He extracted boxes from behind the counter.

' . . . so you sell a lot of these gloves? To other customers?'

'Not a great many, miss. These are a speciality.'

'You wouldn't have a record of those who buy them?'

The man pursed his lips. 'Not as a rule, miss. Not to offend, but we don't share our customers' private information.'

A board creaked behind Rose. Someone, she thought, had just ducked behind the shelves. Her spine prickled.

'I'd like to buy a pair for my father,' she told the man. 'I'm sure these are the correct size.'

While she paid for them, she stole a glance behind the shelves. Whoever had been lurking there had gone.

Rose left the shop and walked back down the Shudders, her mind racing.

Silvercrest Hall? She had never heard of the place. But Argyle had been a butler! He must have known of its existence. She would go to Ravensgate, and—

'Ow!'

Lost in her musings, she had tripped over someone. A beggar in a tattered coat, eyes blazing above cavernous cheeks. Gin fumes filled the air. 'Watch your step, girl!' he rasped.

'I beg your pardon.' Scarlet-faced, Rose dug in her purse for alms. 'My mind was elsewhere.'

He snorted. 'Lost, eh?'

'I'm – no, not exactly. I'm just looking into something.' Rose saw people stare at her as they passed – young ladies weren't supposed to stop and talk to beggars. A well-dressed gentleman curled his lip and muttered something about 'vermin'.

'You couldn't help, I'm afraid,' Rose added.

The beggar looked indignant. 'I know plenty of secrets, miss! Keep me eyes peeled.'

Rose cleared her throat. 'Well, then . . . do you know of Silvercrest Hall?'

The beggar spat.

'I know it,' he snarled. 'Wouldn't go near it!'

Rose stared at him. 'Why ever not?'

The man looked away. A police constable appeared at the corner of the street. Several shop-owners started muttering to him.

Rose held out her freshly-wrapped package.

'Gloves,' she said.

The beggar stared at her suspiciously.

'Gloves. They're new. Please take them. It's not a bribe. It's a gift.'

Slowly, he reached for the package and opened it. A boy pushing a wheelbarrow gave Rose a bemused smile.

'I hope they fit,' said Rose.

There was a long moment while the beggar scratched at his beard. He cleared his throat.

'Not to be ungrateful,' he said. 'But this ain't funny. You asked me about Silvercrest Hall, and gave me these? Black gloves? What are you tryin' to put over me?'

Rose blinked in astonishment. 'I, no . . . I'm sorry. I didn't mean to offend you.'

'I see them walk past,' he muttered. 'Pretend

not to see me. Treat me like scum. Threw me out, they did. Like I was dirt.'

'That – was unkind,' said Rose faintly. She had no idea who he was talking about.

'And now the cats are disappearin'. Oh, I know what he's up to.'

Rose started. The cats? What did he know about them? Heddsworth had mentioned the statues, and now . . .

'He thinks I don't see – but I was there.' He whispered. 'I saw.'

'What?' Rose leaned closer. 'You saw—'

'Oi!' The police constable strode up. 'You stinking old soak – get away from her!'

'Ain't doing no 'arm,' whined the beggar.

'He's not bothering—' began Rose.

'He's a disgrace,' snapped the constable. 'Pestering decent folk.' He turned back to the beggar. 'I'm watching you – behave, or you'll end up in the clink.'

Scowling, the beggar let himself be escorted off

by the constable. Passers-by were staring. Rose walked reluctantly away.

Rose was on her way to Ravensgate when a carriage rolled to a stop beside her.

'Rose!' cried Emily Proops from the window. 'Oh, I've been longing to talk to you! Ever since you sent me that note about the man in the graveyard! You must come home with me and tell me all about it.'

'But—' was all Rose got out before the driver whisked her into the carriage. Emily kept up an excited monologue until they reached her home. The front door opened, and Rose beheld Emily's intimidating butler, Spillwell.

She had always been unnerved by his spectral appearance. A long nose, white hair, deep-set black eyes. His starched collar had rubbed his neck an angry shade of red.

'Miss Raventhorpe,' he said icily.

'Good morning.' Rose forced a smile.

Emily greeted Spillwell, whirled past in a mass of black skirts, and dragged Rose indoors to the sitting-room sofa. 'So, your father left for the Far East?'

'Yes,' said Rose. 'He felt very badly about it, having to leave right after Argyle's funeral. He was going to take Argyle with him. But there wasn't time to find another butler, and I can't imagine how he could bear to, now.'

'Do you need to borrow any mourning clothes? I have a beautiful black shawl. Castilian. And a cape, edged with sable. Well, not sable exactly, it's dyed fox fur, but you can hardly tell the difference . . . '

'No, no, thank you, Emily. I wondered if—'

'. . . Or I could lend you my tear-catcher bottle. And my book of tragic poetry. There's a wonderful ode to a dead canary. I'm going to recite it at the Young Ladies' Poetry Society.'

Rose dropped her voice. 'Emily – how did Spillwell react to the news about Argyle?'

'Spillwell?' Emily blinked. 'Oh, he never said a word. Father put a poker in the umbrella-stand to fight burglars with, and we've locked up all our silver. But Spillwell doesn't seem all that troubled. It's most peculiar. Especially after what you told me about that strange butler man.'

'There have been three butler stabbings,' said Rose. 'And three cat statues disappearing. I think they're connected.' She toyed with her hat. 'In fact, I'm beginning to think someone means to kill all the butlers in Yorke.'

'All of them?' said Emily, in disbelief. 'Why?'

'I don't know. It's something to do with the black gloves, and maybe a place called Silvercrest Hall. Have you heard of it?'

'No – but what about that mystery butler? I mean, you said he had a sword . . . '

Emily stopped. Spillwell had entered the room, bearing a tray of strawberry-cream tarts. He set out an antique Georgian sugar bowl, and began to pour tea from the silver teapot.

'Excuse me, Spillwell,' Rose said carefully. 'Would you happen to know of a butler named Heddsworth?'

Spillwell's hands remained perfectly steady.

'Heddsworth? I am afraid not, Miss Raventhorpe.'

'Or a place named Silvercrest Hall?'

'An academy for butlers, miss. Very respectable, I understand, but I am not well acquainted with it.'

He set down the teapot, and picked up the tray. As he did so his coat-cuff pulled back, revealing his right wrist. It bore a long, thin scar.

Rose choked on her tea.

'Did you have an accident?' she asked, pointing to the scar.

Spillwell smoothed the cuff back down. 'I don't recall, Miss Raventhorpe.'

'But it must have hurt.'

'I have had the occasional accident. I assure you it is nothing. Is that all, Miss Emily?'

'Oh yes. Thank you.'

He left the room.

'You see?' Emily beamed. 'There's absolutely nothing to worry about!'

Rose walked back to the Shudders at a brisk pace. She was brimming with irritation at Spillwell. He must know all about Silvercrest Hall!

She would talk to that beggar again. Rose glanced up automatically at the place where the cat statue had been, and her heart twinged. She missed Argyle terribly.

Pulling herself together, she went to where she had last seen the beggar. The place was strewn with rubbish, and she had to squint to see him. Little more than a lump, curled on a pile of rags. She approached, and bent cautiously over him.

'I'm sorry to bother you again,' she whispered. 'I wondered if you could tell me more about the Hall. If you know.'

There was no answer. She touched his shoulder.

The beggar rolled over like a sack of potatoes.

Rose stared in horror at the dark, sticky pool of blood on the ground. At his face – his blank, staring eyes . . .

Someone seized her by the arm, and dragged her deeper into the alleyway. A gleaming blade lifted. Rose was about to scream but . . .

'Miss Raventhorpe,' said a voice at her ear, 'you are positively beginning to frighten me.'

Chapter 5

The Guardians of Yorke

'*I've* frightened *you*?'

Rose caught the scent of silver polish and tea. She turned around to see her assailant – Heddsworth – looking tense. He lowered his rapier, and she saw he carried a walking stick today instead of an umbrella.

'Quiet. Don't draw people's attention.' He drew her away from the body of the murdered beggar. Rose glanced again at the terrible sight. She pulled away from Heddsworth.

'But he's dead! He's been—'

Heddsworth slid the rapier into the walking stick. He took hold of her arm, walking her away from the scene, into the flow of people. Another police constable was strolling in their direction. 'Slowly now. Before anyone notices. You mustn't be seen here.'

'Let me go!'

Exasperation crept into his voice. 'Miss Raventhorpe, don't you realise what has happened? This is the Black Glove's work.'

She looked back at the corpse, horrified. The police constable had discovered the beggar's body. He covered it with a tattered blanket.

Rose turned to Heddsworth, close to tears.

'Why would anyone kill an old beggar?'

'That old beggar was a butler once,' said Heddsworth, and a muscle twitched in his cheek. His voice wavered a fraction, but he controlled it. 'His name was Herrick.'

'What?'

Another butler! Rose felt dazed. And his name . . . she had never even thought to ask his name . . .

'He drank,' said Heddsworth. 'Which is a shame, because he was a promising butler to start with. One of the Hall's best students. Excellent swordsman. But one day he made a terrible mistake while serving dinner to guests – dropped a lobster into a duchess's lap. It shattered his nerves. He took to drinking, which made things worse. That's what he came to, poor fellow. Blamed the Hall for throwing him out, but he was in no state to hold down any job by then.'

'Oh, I see,' said Rose. 'So if you're a butler in Yorke, even an ex-butler, you're bound to be killed! Or disgraced, or chased by bodysnatchers—'

'Hush.'

Rose whirled around, pale with outrage.

'How can I be sure you're not the murderer? You were there!'

His calm blue eyes met hers. 'I promise you,

Miss Raventhorpe, I am the safest person for you to be with right now.'

'How can I believe *that*?' Rose demanded.

'You deserve an explanation,' said Heddsworth. 'And you will have one. But you will have to trust me.'

Rose huffed out a breath. 'We'll see,' she muttered, but, all the same, she followed him down the broad street of Riversgate, across Parksgate, around the cathedral and over the bridge. They entered the park, where nurses watched children sail boats on the lake, and hurried down the Long Walk, passing all its statues. Then they struck off the path, entering a thicket of trees.

Heddsworth stopped suddenly. Rose halted alongside. 'What is it?' she hissed between clenched teeth. The butler gave a small shake of the head, urging her to stay quiet.

Two people emerged from the trees. A man with a limp, and a determined-looking young woman. The young man's uneven gait made him thump the ground in an ungainly manner as he walked, forced to favour his good leg.

The woman walked slowly so as not to outpace him, but retained an independent air. They might have been a couple out for a morning's stroll. However, the man leaned on a walking stick that would easily accommodate a rapier. The woman had a long pocket in her dress, the sort meant to carry a fan or a parasol. The hilt of a rapier was visible at the top.

'Good Lord, Heddsworth, why have you brought her?' demanded the woman, as they drew near. 'Miss Regemont will go berserk!'

'It was necessary, Bronson,' said Heddsworth. 'Miss Raventhorpe, meet Bronson, a butler of Silvercrest Hall. Do not call her a housekeeper, unless you desire a duel at dawn.'

Bronson glowered. 'If you don't tell us what's going on, I'm going to duel you in broad daylight!'

'Now, now,' said the young man. 'Play nicely

together.' He had wheat-gold hair, a cleft in his firm chin and blue eyes that sparkled like the sea. He bowed gallantly to Rose. 'Charlie Malone. Delighted to make your acquaintance.'

Rose was too surprised to do anything but nod.

'So what happened?' asked Charlie.

'Herrick,' said Heddsworth, briefly. 'Stabbed to death.'

Bronson's knuckles whitened. Charlie's cheerful face turned grim. 'Poor old boy,' he muttered.

'Miss Raventhorpe found him. I thought it imperative to get her away.'

Bronson was pacing, her skirts swishing against laced boots. 'Sweet Saint Iphigenia, Heddsworth – what's to be done?'

'That is for the Hall to decide,' said Heddsworth. 'We'd better take Miss Raventhorpe with us, via the Stairs Below.'

'The what?' said Rose.

'It's a – a shortcut,' said Heddsworth. 'Well,

perhaps not a shortcut, but an alternative means of getting to Silvercrest Hall.'

'Heddsworth!' Bronson sounded shocked. 'The Stairs Below! We've never taken an outsider in there.'

'Today we must make an exception,' said Heddsworth. 'We can trust Miss Raventhorpe. Argyle was her butler. She can help us.'

'Help us how?' Bronson demanded. 'What's she going to do – embroider cushions with inspiring quotations?'

Rose glared at her. 'I can help! He was my friend too.'

'Friend?' said Bronson sceptically. Rose ignored her.

'We'll go to the nearest door,' said Heddsworth. 'And use my key.'

Rose followed the little group. 'So,' she said, 'Argyle was a swordsman, like all of you? Did he actually duel people?'

'Oh yes,' said Heddsworth. 'He was a master.

We don't learn just for self-defence, or exercise. Butlers love a good duel.'

'With swords?' Rose asked. 'And pistols?'

'Yes,' said Heddsworth. 'We duel mostly to settle matters of honour. Rarely to the death, mind you. Some duels are over the proper laying of a tablecloth.'

'I can't stand badly placed tablecloths, myself,' said Bronson, hand on her rapier hilt.

'And we use our skills to protect the city,' said Heddsworth. 'In fighting bodysnatchers, for example. But that side of the Hall is a secret. Few know we are the Guardians of Yorke.'

'I – I never knew Argyle did any such thing,' said Rose, flabbergasted.

'Well, he wouldn't have whipped out a rapier at the breakfast table,' said Charlie cheerfully. 'We have to be discreet. But I saw him fight with the best – and win. You should be proud, Miss Raventhorpe. Your butler could draw his sword in the same time it took most people to draw breath.'

'Where is his sword now?' Rose asked. If her beloved butler really was a swordsman, she wanted to see the evidence.

'We saw to it that Argyle's sword was buried with him,' Charlie said. 'As befits a Guardian.'

Rose nodded, thinking again. 'So it's not a secret that there is a butlers' academy, but it is a secret that the butlers are trained to be the Guardians of Yorke,' she said, determined to keep up. 'A kind of brotherhood?'

'Correct,' said Heddsworth over his shoulder. 'Herrick the beggar was one of our own, once. We shall see to it that he gets a decent burial.'

Rose adjusted her pace to Charlie's limp. He must have sensed her curiosity, for he murmured, 'Took a hit to the leg once with a sharpener – rapier, I mean. Stuck with it, I'm afraid. I tell most people it was a cricket injury.'

'You were injured with a rapier? What happened?'

'I was on patrol alone in the graveyard. Rather

reckless of me, I'm afraid. Dark night, and a gang of Crows attacked. Took a hit to the leg before I managed to get away.'

Rose fumbled for something to say. 'I – I'm sure you're still a good butler.'

'Oh, I'm not a proper one, not any more. Can't have it, you see, a limping butler. How would you carry the trays? Walk quietly downstairs to wind the clocks? Not a suitable job for me, not now. But I still have a job. I work at the Hall. Miss Regemont insisted.'

'Who is—'

'Charlie, you've a mouth like a badly run circus,' snapped Bronson from up ahead. 'You'd let anything escape.'

'What an impressive simile,' whispered Charlie. 'Bet she thought about that one for days.'

Rose twisted her cameo in her fingers. 'Why was Argyle so upset that the cat statues disappeared? Was it because of the prophecy?'

'You shouldn't tell her,' protested Bronson.

Heddsworth glanced about. They were in a quiet part of the park.

'It's because of a legend,' he said quietly. 'According to the story, the founder of the cathedral, Saint Iphigenia, had a great many cats. They would sit on the walls, and prowl around the city at night. One night there was a great thunderstorm. It was so violent that people feared the cathedral and the walls would fall. That the very graveyards would be destroyed, and the dead broken from their tombs.'

Rose shivered.

'Nobody knew what Saint Iphigenia did,' said Heddsworth. 'But in the morning, the city was safe. Her cats had disappeared, but statues of black cats had appeared all over the city.'

'Iphigenia had a son, named Arlington,' Charlie continued. 'He was a shield-bearer to a king, and he built Silvercrest Hall. He decided he would train people devoted to service, and secretly teach them to be Guardians. Iphigenia promised her son that her cat statues would protect his Guardians as long as they remained in the city. Ever since those days, people have claimed that the cat statues have the power to come to life, and protect the city. We believe in that story, and the prophecy about their loss. If the cats start to disappear, it will not only be ruin for Yorke. It will mean the end for us, too.'

Thunder rolled ominously in the darkening sky.

Rose stared at the three butlers, digesting what she had just heard

'So Argyle was shocked when the cats disappeared,' she said slowly, 'because the whole city is threatened. He really believes the loss of the cats will destroy it.'

Heddsworth nodded. 'We are all in dreadful danger if we lose the protection of the statues.'

Rose gasped. Argyle had hidden everything from her. Everything.

They passed the cathedral and entered the street of Parksgate. Heddsworth stopped at an iron door set low in a wall. He looked stealthily around to ensure they were not being observed. Then, from his pocket, he took a small silver key. He opened the door, giving a good shove on its creaking hinges. 'Hmm. Hasn't been used for a while . . . ugh, cobwebs.'

He took a brush from his pocket and swept the cobwebs away. They entered the dark space. Rose could hardly believe it. This door in the street, this dark and dingy tunnel, would take them to Silvercrest Hall . . .

Bronson shut the door, and the dark became absolute. Heddsworth struck a match.

'Mind the steps,' he said.

They walked cautiously down a set of narrow stone stairs. The first thing Rose noticed was the drop in temperature. Then the sound of dripping water. Heddsworth's dwindling match showed a row of lanterns hanging on the wall. He took one and lit it. Rose rubbed her cold arms.

'How long has this place been here?' she asked. 'Did the butlers dig out all the tunnels?'

'Oh no. The Stairs Below are ancient,' said Heddsworth. 'Been here since Roman times, if not earlier.' He placed his silver key in her palm. 'This is an Infinity Key. It opens every door to the Stairs.'

Rose inspected the key by the lantern-light. The teeth of the key were shaped like a tiny maze, while an intricate filigree cat sat on its top.

'No one can easily duplicate that,' said Heddsworth. 'It would take a master locksmith.'

'Why is it called an Infinity Key?'

'Because,' said Charlie Malone, 'legend has it that there are an infinity of doors. And if you get lost in here, you're stuck for eternity.'

Rose shuddered.

They started down the tunnel. Rose hoped Heddsworth had a good sense of direction.

'How many people know about this place?'

'We butlers all have keys,' said Heddsworth. 'Mind your head, Miss Raventhorpe, there's a low bit of brickwork . . . Butlers need to be quick and efficient, and this helps us get about Yorke. You'd be surprised at the buildings these passages lead to. I myself am not certain of all of them.'

'I suppose it does help you as butlers,' Rose said. 'Being able to move around the city unseen, no matter what the weather.'

'It does,' said Bronson. 'A pity it doesn't help me keep a position. The only situation I can obtain is as a housekeeper. And then I get fired.'

'Why?' asked Rose, shocked.

Heddsworth cleared his throat. 'She ends up telling the household butler what to do, and if he so much as polishes the forks badly she challenges him to a duel.'

'Oh,' said Rose.

'But then, it was a struggle even to convince Miss Regemont to enrol me as a student,' said Bronson, scowling in the lantern-light. 'There'd never been a female student at the Hall before. Miss Regemont is the head of Hall, not a butler.'

'So how did you become a student?' Rose asked.

'Oh, Bronson saved my life,' said Heddsworth.

'Really?'

'I was fighting a number of ruffians,' explained Heddsworth. 'And she came to my assistance. Bronson has always been good with a blade. Learned from her father. A vicar who liked fencing. At any rate, I insisted she be taken on as a student. Miss Regemont agreed, but she also made Bronson undertake some ordeals. She had already proved herself in combat, but had to serve at the table for a maharaja, who kept five tigers in the dining room. Then she spent an entire day at the Hall at everyone's beck and call. While keeping her temper, naturally. Once she passed those trials, she was accepted as a student.'

'Oh, well done!' Rose was deeply impressed.

They walked on. A fall of rain had affected one passage, and the ground was thick with mud. It smelled of rotting rushes and the River Knoll.

'Not that way,' said Heddsworth, guiding Rose

down the main tunnel. 'There are sections that aren't safe.'

Rose thought of what might happen in such passageways. A bead of sweat trickled down her back and she shivered, pulling her cloak more tightly around her shoulders.

Suddenly she had an uneasy feeling of being followed. She looked back and saw a flash of white in the dark. She gasped.

'Someone's there!'

The butlers drew their swords. Heddsworth lifted the lantern.

The stranger, carrying his own lantern, was wearing a cloak, and had a hat pulled low over his face. He also carried a rapier. In the dim light, Rose saw dark stains on the blade.

'It's him,' gasped Bronson. 'Herrick's murderer!'

Bronson rushed forward. The stranger bolted down another passageway. His lantern-light faded. His footsteps grew fainter. Rose's heart galloped at the thought of being that close to the Black Glove.

Bronson came back, a picture of fury.

'He got away,' she said bitterly. 'He got away!'

'Yes,' said Heddsworth, through gritted teeth. 'But we saw him. Did anyone recognise him?'

'I didn't see his face,' said Rose.

'If he was in the Stairs Below, we know something definite about him,' whispered Charlie. 'He has an Infinity Key.'

Chapter 6

Miss Regemont

'Here we are,' said Heddsworth. 'The door to Silvercrest Hall.'

High on the wall Rose glimpsed words carved into a silvery crest:

Et gladio et polies

Rose's brow furrowed. 'With sword and polish,' she translated.

Heddsworth smiled, and held the door open for her. 'Welcome to the butlers' academy.'

Waterfall chandeliers dazzled. Mirrors sparkled. Gilt chairs gleamed. Every surface had been polished and dusted. The room looked ready for a ball, complete with waltzes, champagne and a symphony orchestra. A stately woman in a crimson gown was walking around with a white glove on one hand, inspecting the surfaces for dust.

Rose noticed embroidered silver patterns around the lady's hem and sleeves, reminding her of crossed rapiers. The woman's steel-grey hair was coiffed in a pompadour, and her dark eyes glittered at the new arrivals.

'Ah, Heddsworth,' she said. 'I see we have an unexpected guest. May I ask why have you brought her here? And by the Stairs Below?'

Rose bristled. She was there to help find the murderer!

'I beg your pardon, madam,' said Heddsworth. 'There were extraordinary circumstances.' He turned to Rose. 'Miss Raventhorpe, this is Miss

Regemont – descendant of our founder, and head of the Hall.'

Miss Regemont gave Rose a cool nod. 'I am most sorry for the loss of your butler, Miss Raventhorpe. A good man. But we need to discuss urgent matters, so . . . '

'I know it is breaking our rules, madam, but I believe Miss Raventhorpe should stay,' said Heddsworth. 'The young lady was close to Argyle. She is willing to help us.'

'Close?' said Miss Regemont dubiously. 'You mean, on friendly terms?'

'Yes,' said Rose. 'All my life. He used to iron my nappies.'

There was a stunned silence.

'Well,' said Bronson. 'I never pictured Argyle as a nursemaid.'

Rose glared. 'I was at the scene when Argyle was murdered. Right on our doorstep. And other butlers have been killed, and the cat statues are disappearing.' She turned to Miss Regemont.

'Whether there is a curse on the city or not, I'm sure the murderer is planning to kill again. He's just murdered Herrick the beggar!'

Miss Regemont paled.

'Herrick? The poor man has not buttled for donkey's years. Why would anyone murder him?'

'We do not know, madam,' said Heddsworth. 'But we saw a suspicious person in the Stairs Below, just now. A man with a bloodstained rapier. We fear it was the Black Glove, and he has an Infinity Key.'

Miss Regemont's eyes flashed. 'If Herrick is dead . . . please tell me you have his Infinity Key safe!'

Heddsworth looked taken aback. 'I – I did not check, madam. I needed to get Miss Raventhorpe away from the scene. Madam, do you mean that Herrick never returned his Infinity Key, after he was expelled from the Hall?'

'I could not bear to take it from him.' Miss Regemont wrung her hands. 'Usually I insist they are turned in, once a butler is dismissed from service, or if they die. Perhaps it was wrong of me to allow Herrick to keep his – but I never thought it would come to this! He kept that key hidden on him. If one of the Crows killed him, they could have stolen his key and used it to escape into the Stairs Below.' She paused. 'This calls for desperate measures. I do not want anyone to take unnecessary risks. You are all to stay out of the Stairs Below.'

Heddsworth looked taken aback. 'Madam?'

'The Stairs Below must be banned to all butlers indefinitely. I trust you will all obey. Otherwise I shall insist on your turning in your Infinity Keys.'

Charlie Malone winced. 'But what are we to do then, madam? Four of our number are dead.'

'We shall investigate,' declared Miss Regemont. 'We shall discover the identity of this fiend, and bring him to justice.'

'We will,' said Rose. 'I can help.'

'Honestly, this is—' began Bronson.

'I say we give Miss Raventhorpe a chance to prove herself,' said Heddsworth. 'She's clever and brave, and resourceful, and knows the city well.'

'I do,' said Rose. 'Argyle made sure I knew my way around Yorke.'

Miss Regemont gave her a long look. 'Very well. In a time of crisis we should accept offers of help. We should go to where Herrick was murdered, and search for clues.'

'I agree,' said Rose. She glanced at Bronson, as if daring her to protest.

The young woman sighed. 'Oh, all right. We can take a Hall carriage back to the Shudders. All of us.'

It was quieter at the Shudders now, a breeze whipping rubbish and leaves across the cobbles. Leaving the carriage, Rose and her friends hurried to the place where Herrick had been stabbed. It was at the entrance to a skitterway, as the alleys in Yorke were called.

The place looked deserted now – nobody would even know Herrick had been killed there. The police constables had already removed his body.

Heddsworth walked carefully around the rags and debris. He picked up an empty gin bottle, and sniffed it. 'Phew,' he said, wincing. 'That makes the eyes water.'

'What a place to live,' said Bronson. 'Ugh, this blanket – riddled with fleas! To think he used to be a butler . . . I wish we could have helped him.'

Rose pushed an empty gin bottle aside, and pounced on a creamy white feather. 'I've seen something like this before!' she exclaimed. 'That Crow woman, Miss Deacon at the cemetery, wore a hat with a white feather.'

'I knew it!' said Bronson. 'Those thieving murderers!'

'It must have been one of them we saw in the Stairs Below,' agreed Charlie Malone.

Rose saw the glint of silver. Gingerly she picked up a shabby broken chain. 'What's this?'

'May I see?' said Heddsworth.

She showed him the chain. The others came to look.

'Aha!' said Miss Regemont. 'That chain held Herrick's Infinity Key. Is there any chance it is still here?'

They all searched diligently, but there was no sign of a key in the skitterway.

'Then we were right,' said Charlie Malone dispiritedly. 'The murderer stole the key.'

Rose fiddled with her cameo, turning it over in her fingers.

'Let's go to the Pavilion tearooms,' Charlie suggested. 'I think we could all use a cup of tea.'

He offered his arm to Rose, who took it. Heddsworth took Bronson's arm, and Miss Regemont sailed elegantly forth in the lead.

The tearooms were built like an ornate white basket. The butlers took a table in the garden, and admired the quality of the silver cutlery. They ate crisp, caramel-topped eclairs, scones with elderflower cream and cherry shortbread.

Miss Regemont sipped her tea and frowned. 'Four butlers have been killed. Four! Tremayne, Guillaume, Argyle and now Herrick. Who will be struck down next?'

'If we think it's the Crows,' said Rose, 'why don't we tell the police?'

'We need solid evidence,' said Miss Regemont. 'Especially as some policemen turn a blind eye to grave-robbery.'

Rose bit her lip. 'Is there any reason why the Crows would have attacked those particular victims first?'

Miss Regemont shook her head.

'I cannot think why. They rarely patrolled in the graveyard. Guillaume worked for an elderly countess. He was courting the housekeeper, and asked me for a character reference and a book on etiquette. Tremayne was employed by a composer, and did a lot of travelling. He excelled at learning languages. I had to update his references regarding the improvement of his fencing skills.'

'Their employers liked them, then?' asked Rose. She took a bite of cucumber sandwich.

'Certainly, Miss Raventhorpe. I have no suspicion of their employers. They trusted their butlers implicitly. You need to, after all. A butler is in a position of great responsibility.'

'There's something else I was wondering,' said Rose. 'Could any of the murders have been for money?'

'Most unlikely,' said Miss Regemont, wrinkling her nose over her teacup. The other butlers nodded agreement. 'Tremayne and Guillaume were not wealthy, and I can't see how a murderer would get anything they left. They both had rapiers, but those were not stolen. And I doubt Herrick had a penny to his name.'

'Argyle was not rich either,' Rose admitted. 'In his will, he left most of his savings to charity.'

'Did Argyle leave any helpful documents?' asked Miss Regemont. 'Letters, accounts, keepsakes?'

'No,' said Rose. 'I checked.'

'Miss Regemont,' said Heddsworth exasperatedly. 'I commend your compassion, but have you let your soft heart get the better of you on other occasions? Do any other ex-butlers still have their keys?'

'Only one,' retorted Miss Regemont. 'Harry Dodge, the magician. We need to warn him not to use the Stairs Below.'

'The magician?' asked Rose.

'He was a student butler once at the Hall,' Charlie Malone explained. 'But he preferred performing magic tricks to buttling. One night he was spotted performing onstage at a theatre, and Miss Regemont expelled him.'

'I had to,' said Miss Regemont stiffly. 'It was

perfectly clear the man was not cut out for the life of a Silvercrest Hall butler. I let him keep his Infinity Key, and he swore he would look after it purely as a memento.'

'Too charming for his own good, if you ask me,' muttered Bronson.

Rose frowned. 'So he has a key. Couldn't he be a suspect, if he has a grudge against you?'

Miss Regemont shook her head. 'Why on earth would he do such a thing? He seems to be doing well in his theatre act. His show is hugely popular at the Clarion, and that gives him an alibi – he couldn't commit murder while working onstage. And he would hardly need to steal Herrick's key, when he has his own.'

Rose nibbled at a piece of shortbread. 'I could attend his performance tonight. I have a friend who would love to come with me. Then I could warn him about the Stairs Below.' *And ask him whether he still bears a grudge,* she added in her head.

'That would be kind of you, Miss Raventhorpe,'

said Miss Regemont. 'He may bear us no ill will, but I suspect he would not like one of us telling him what to do.'

'What shall we do about the cat statues?' Bronson wanted to know. 'We need to think of the prophecy. Should we take them down for safekeeping, or put a watch on them?'

'If we let them stay, we might catch the thief in the act,' suggested Charlie Malone. 'Besides, we're the Guardians of Yorke. We mustn't show the murderer we are intimidated.'

'I agree. We should investigate the Crows,' said Heddsworth. 'If they are the murderers, we need to find evidence as soon as possible.'

'But they live in the Muckyards. We can't let Miss Raventhorpe go there,' argued Bronson.

Heddsworth saw Rose's crestfallen expression. 'You come with me to Locks and Clocks, Miss Raventhorpe. If the Crows now possess an Infinity Key, they will want to make copies for each of them, and only one person we know can do that.'

Rose twirled her cameo again in her fingers. The words of the prophecy came to mind. *The dead will rise up from their graves . . .*

'They won't,' she said under her breath. 'We're going to stop them.'

Chapter 7

The Butler Magician

Rose counted the cat statues on the way to Locks and Clocks. There was the familiar statue above Dorabella's, drinking from a teacup ... the cat statue balancing on a chimney pot ... the statue peering down at the fishmonger's display.

And one empty space.

The statue that had used to be above the tailor's – a cat playing with a ball of wool – was gone. Rose felt Heddsworth tense beside her. He had noticed too.

Gritting her teeth, Rose opened the door to Locks and Clocks. Its wrought iron sign was of a dragon dangling an elaborate key from its jaws. A window display showed revolving golden cogs and wheels.

The shop was full of carriage clocks, grandfather clocks, pocket watches no bigger than buttons and timepieces shaped like carousels, which chimed and moved on the hour. Beautiful jewellery reposed in cases. A Yorke bracelet sparkled with a setting of ruby, opal, sapphire and emerald: the first letters spelling out 'r-o-s-e', for the floral emblem of Yorkesborough.

The jeweller was Mr Samuel Goldsmith. His daughters, Sapphire and Garnet, waited on them. Sapphire, the prettiest, chatted to the customers. Garnet, who was plain, polished a display cabinet.

'Good morning,' said Garnet, to Rose. 'May I help you? Jewellery, perhaps?'

'No thank you,' said Rose. 'I was waiting to meet someone. Do you make jewellery yourself?'

Garnet's mouth fell open.

'Me, miss?' she sputtered. 'Father does the work, not me!'

'Oh,' said Rose. She pointed to a bracelet on Garnet's wrist. 'It's only that I thought that was an interesting choice of jewellery.'

It was a charm bracelet, but instead of the usual charms, it held a tiny silver pair of pliers, an anvil, a hammer and a clock face.

Reddening, Garnet closed her hand around the bracelet. 'Pardon me, but that is none of your business, miss.'

'I'm sorry,' said Rose. 'I mean, I'd love to make jewellery. It must be hard work.'

'It's what the Goldsmiths do,' said Garnet. 'The men, anyway,' she added sourly. 'We girls are supposed to be nice and charming and sell things.' Suddenly she reached out and tapped Rose's cameo. 'Oh!' she said in sudden astonishment. 'It was for you.'

Rose lifted the cameo from her neck. 'You mean this? Argyle had it made here?'

'Yes,' said Garnet. She smiled at the cameo, and brushed it with a fingertip. 'Interesting work. We've never made one quite like that before.'

'With a cat on it, you mean?'

Garnet only smiled. 'I think your friend wants your attention.'

Rose turned to see Heddsworth beckoning. 'The Infinity Keys were all crafted by hand, like pieces of jewellery,' he told Rose in a low voice. 'It was Carmenthius, a friend of our founder Arlington, who fitted all those locks and made all those keys, for the Stairs Below. A lifetime's work. Only one jeweller I know could make an Infinity Key, let alone copy one.' He turned to Sapphire. 'I would like to speak to Mr Goldsmith, please.'

'I'll fetch him, sir.'

Mr Goldsmith duly appeared. He had grey curls and several gold teeth that flashed when he smiled. 'Ah, Mr Heddsworth,' he said. 'And a young friend.' He bowed to Rose. 'What can I do for you?'

'This is Miss Raventhorpe,' said Heddsworth.

'Perhaps we could have a private discussion?'

Mr Goldsmith nodded. 'Certainly, sir. Do come into my office.'

They followed him behind the counter, and through a door into a workshop. The bench was covered with pliers, anvils and hammers.

'Whenever we need any work done on our keys,' Heddsworth explained to Rose, 'we ask Mr Goldsmith. He's the descendent of Carmenthius, the original key-maker.'

'We do our best to uphold his legacy,' said Mr Goldsmith proudly. 'How may I help you, sir?'

Heddsworth took his own Infinity Key from a chain around his neck.

'Ah! A beautiful piece of work!' Mr Goldsmith admired the key. 'And a very old one, too.'

'Indeed. Not easy to copy. I understand?'

'No, not at all. It would take weeks of work.' Mr Goldsmith frowned. 'Do you require a copy, sir?'

'We only thought,' said Rose quickly, 'that it would help to know. In case this one ever got lost.'

My Goldsmith's brow frowned. 'Well it's not just any key, miss. It's an Infinity Key. I couldn't make a copy just like that.'

'I suppose you haven't for years,' Heddsworth suggested.

'That I haven't, sir.' The jewellery gave a reverent smile. 'I have to ask permission of Miss Regemont, you know, whenever I make another Key for the Hall.'

'Quite right,' said Heddsworth. 'That is good to know. A pleasure to visit the shop, Mr Goldsmith.' He nodded to Rose. 'We should go now, Miss Raventhorpe.'

They left the shop. 'That is a relief, at least,' said Heddsworth. 'But there is still a missing key out there. Now, I must help the others look for the Crows. Will you be all right attending the theatre, Miss Raventhorpe?'

'Oh yes, it's no trouble at all,' said Rose, and crossed her fingers behind her back.

*

Emily Proops leaned perilously far out over the balcony. 'I can't believe we're somewhere so scandalous!'

'Shhh,' hissed Rose. 'If Mother finds out, we're doomed.'

Emily had provided the necessary alibi for their outing, telling her mother she wanted to place flowers on her dog's grave. Having dressed in her oldest clothes, Rose had pleaded with Emily to wear simple attire. That way they would avoid unwanted attention, and be comfortable in the stuffy theatre. Emily had argued ('It's the theatre, Rose! One must dress for dramatics!') and was now attired in a ruffled black lace dress and a heavily veiled hat.

'Sometimes, Emily,' Rose told her, 'I think you should have been an ancient Egyptian. They took funeral matters terribly seriously.'

'Bertram would have liked to have been embalmed,' said Emily, with a smile.

The girls sat in box seats of worn plush, flanked

by potted ferns. The audience chattered noisily. There were shopgirls giggling with their friends, and young workmen who grinned and winked at them. Elderly people squinted at programmes and craned their necks to see the orchestra. 'Lor,' Rose heard one man say. 'They got a pianer, Dorrie. A real pianer, and a fiddle and all!'

No wonder, Rose thought, that Lady Constance disapproved of the Clarion. She was grateful her mother was in London, posing for a portrait. Rose had received a brief note from her, reminding Rose to practice her piano and table etiquette.

Rose had hesitated about taking a box, but she was determined to see everything onstage. She knew little of Dodge, the butler-turned-magician. She wanted to know more about him.

'It was good of you to come, Emily,' Rose added. 'I didn't think you would attend a theatre.'

'The theatre is balm for the afflicted soul,' said Emily, gripping her black lace handkerchief. 'And there is a wonderfully tragic song after the interval,' she added, flicking through the programme. She straightened her hat and patted her hair, which was done in a style called Dying Poet.

The orchestra struck up, and the curtains swished apart. Jugglers, dancers, fire-eaters and comic singers took over the stage. A knife-thrower hurled glittering knives around his sweating assistant. Six acrobats in purple tights balanced on balls and chairs. An athletic girl did a tightrope act, waving to the audience before she shinned back down the rope.

Then came the announcement. 'The sensation of the Clarion – the conjuror of a thousand tricks – the Master of Mysteries!'

A silvery spotlight illuminated the stage. Rose leaned forward. The Master of Mysteries stood there, cloaked, masked and impressively silent.

'Ladies and gentlemen,' he began, in a deep, hypnotic voice. 'I am the Master of Mysteries. The Sultan of Secrets. The Emperor of the Unexpected! Tonight we will consort with the spirits of the Netherworld.'

The footlights flickered. Emily clutched her tear-catcher bottle.

Rose narrowed her eyes at the man in the spotlight. Had he really been a butler once? He seemed so – so theatrical, so confident onstage. Weren't butlers supposed to stay in the background?

The magician spun silver balls in his hands. The spheres seemed to dance with a life of their own. He swept a cape over a chair, and the chair disappeared. He poured wine from one crystal goblet to another, and the wine changed colour in midair. A lighted chandelier travelled across the stage, apparently lifted by a wave of his arm. The audience was entranced.

'He's very good at sleight of hand,' whispered Rose.

'Oh, no!' Emily breathed. 'I believe he's consorting with the spirits of the Netherworld.'

'Now,' intoned the magician, 'for my most famous act. The Bodysnatch Trick.'

'Ooooh,' breathed the audience. They leaned forward almost as one.

The lights dropped even lower. Stagehands wheeled in a heavily chained and padlocked box. The magician swirled his scarlet-lined cape, and paced back and forth. He gazed at the audience with burning intensity, and his voice dropped even deeper.

'This is a dangerous trick, ladies and gentlemen.' He lifted his masked face, eyes flashing, and put his hands to his temples. 'It requires great concentration! Every last drop of my energy!' He pointed dramatically to the box.

'For I shall be shut inside this box!' The audience members jumped. He paced the stage, his cape swirling. 'Not only will the box be locked, but members of the audience shall guard the exits to this theatre. Every possible means of escape will be barred. And I shall escape its confines, and appear again before you! Who . . . ' He dropped to one knee, his voice passionately low. 'Who shall dare to consort with the Netherworld? Who shall volunteer to keep watch?'

There was a great showing of hands. The volunteers were chosen, and climbed self-consciously onstage. The magician gestured. 'Take your places as you see fit. You must not let me pass! Call out if you see me. I give you full leave to block my way.'

The atmosphere was thick with anticipation.

'Great spirits of the Netherworld!' cried the Master of Mysteries. 'Give me the wings of invisibility, and the power to cross between the realms of light and darkness!'

Cross the realms of light and darkness? thought Rose scornfully. *He'll be lucky to cross the stage without tripping over that long cape!*

The magician lay down in the box. Stagehands closed the lid, locked the padlocks and fastened a thick rope around it. The orchestra played a drumroll. Audience members whispered frantically. 'What if he don't cross over properly?' 'Sit down, I can't see.' 'He's not going to die, is he, Dorrie? Better cover your eyes, just in case.'

Emily held her hand to her chest. 'Oh, oh, oh,' she whispered. 'I think I'm going to faint.'

Seconds ticked by. The tension stretched. Emily whimpered. Rose wondered, uncomfortably, what happened when a trick like this went wrong.

Suddenly the chains fell off with a clatter. Some women – and not a few men – shrieked. The walls of the box collapsed, showing it to be empty. Everyone gasped. The door to the foyer was flung open.

A man strode down the aisle. His red-lined cape swirled. His eyes sparkled triumphantly behind his mask. He climbed the steps to the stage. Under the spotlight he stood and bowed. There was a great, stunned silence.

Then everyone leapt to their feet, cheering so loudly it shook dust from the chandelier.

Emily jumped up and down, clapping her hands together. 'He's wonderful, truly wonderful!'

Rose watched the magician take his bows. He looked slightly out of breath, but triumphant.

Several ladies in the audience had fainted. Emily glared down at them. 'It's just to get his attention,' she muttered. 'I wouldn't stoop to such a tactic.'

The magician left the stage still bowing to the cheering crowd. The volunteers returned to their seats. It took a while for the audience to calm down enough for the next act to start. The performers, two burly strongmen, did not look happy about it. Rose hoped the magician stayed out of their way.

'We need to go now,' Rose whispered. 'To talk to the magician.'

Emily dug in her reticule for a hand mirror. She turned her head, patting her hairstyle.

'Emily!'

'Yes, all right, I'm coming.'

The girls hurried downstairs, then out through the theatre doors, ducking down the narrow skitterway that led to the back of the building. Here was the backstage door. Rose gingerly turned the handle.

It was locked.

Chapter 8

The Key to a Vanishing Act

Emily fished a black mourning pin from her hair. 'Here,' she whispered. 'See if you can pick the lock.'

'Pick the lock?' said Rose.

'Why not?' said Emily. 'It works in novels.'

Rose inserted the hairpin in the lock and jiggled it.

'I'll stand in front of you,' said Emily, whisking out her handkerchief. 'People avoid disturbing a lady in mourning.'

Rose broke several hairpins before she managed to open the lock. Emily lowered her black parasol to hide them as they slipped through the door.

'Right,' said Rose determinedly. 'We need to look like we belong here.'

A pile of costumes had been left on a chair. Rose swept up an armful of garments and gave a couple to Emily. They dodged ropes, pulleys and bustling stagehands. Performers brushed past, sparkling with sequins and rustling with feathers, smelling of greasepaint and powder.

'Mother would be horrified!' Rose whispered to Emily.

'So would mine,' agreed Emily. 'Father would explode.'

Rose led the way down a corridor, and found the dressing rooms. Each door bore a card with a name on it. 'Domina, Queen of the Tightrope'. 'The Persian Mentalist'. 'The Arabesques'. Then, at last, 'The Master of Mysteries'. Emily stifled a squeal.

Rose shifted the clothes in her arms, and knocked.

'Enter!' said a cheery voice.

Rose opened the door. The room was crowded with black silk hats, capes and playing cards. A dove sat in a cage. The magician, now clad in a crimson dressing-gown, sat at his dressing-table. Stripped of his mask and hat, he now looked an ordinary young man with a headful of raffish curls. He had a copy of *Gothic Poetry* in one hand and a treacle biscuit in the other.

Seeing the young ladies, he stood up at once.

'Well, hello!' he said brightly. 'Unexpected guests!'

Rose put her costumes on a chair, and nudged Emily to do likewise. 'I beg your pardon for intruding. We don't actually work here.'

'Oh, you're admirers?' He grinned at them. 'After my autograph?'

'Yes!' said Emily.

'Er – not exactly,' said Rose. 'I'm Miss Raventhorpe, and this is Miss Proops.'

Dodge bowed to them. 'Please sit down. I see you are in mourning, Miss Proops. My condolences for your loss. A member of the family? A husband?'

'Oh no,' said Emily cheerfully, flinging her veil back. 'It's my dog I am mourning, my darling little Bertram.'

Dodge's eyes lit up. 'He must have been a loyal pet. You are clearly a lady of deep feeling.'

'You are most gallant, sir,' breathed Emily. 'It is a trial I am still endeavouring to overcome.'

Emily and Dodge talked about Gothic poetry. Then about the stage. Then mesmerism. Rose appreciated Emily's efforts to gain Dodge's trust.

'Rose, darling, have you fallen asleep?' said Emily, after ten minutes. 'Terribly sorry, it's so lovely to chat with a nice young man.' She turned to the magician. 'You must think us disgraceful to be here without proper escort, Mr Dodge. I assure you we are not normally so forward. Rose is the Honourable Rose Raventhorpe. Lord Frederick's daughter. She's lovely and clever, can speak all these languages ... oh, and her mother is a celebrated beauty. I keep telling Rose that Her Ladyship should be painted as a Gothic enchantress ... '

Rose wasn't exactly pleased that Emily was telling Dodge so much. *They* were supposed to be investigating *him*.

'If you don't mind, sir, I would like to talk to you about your bodysnatch trick,' Rose broke in. 'How it was done.'

He laughed. 'My dear girl, I can't tell you the details! I've had people offer big money for my secrets. Refused 'em all, of course. Wouldn't do to give away my living.'

'Actually, I think you—'

The magician held up a hand. 'Please, Miss Raventhorpe. I think it's high time we had some tea.' He disappeared behind a screen, and reappeared in a long, buttoned-up velvet tailcoat.

'There. Now I am properly attired.' He swept a hatful of sequins from a table and produced a teapot, cups and a plate of Dorabella's gingerbread cats. Then he poured tea and passed cups to his guests. Emily beamed. Rose poked at a trick box, and found a hidden latch.

'Well, now,' said Dodge comfortably. 'What is your theory, ladies? Do I have an invisible ladder, perhaps? Or a secret accomplice?'

Rose shook her head. 'No. I think it's to do with your past as a butler.'

The magician's smile faltered.

'Well, I – well. I was a butler once.' He waved his cup at her. 'A complete waste of my talents! The stage was the thing for me. Anyway, that has nothing to do with my trick. I don't serve tea and scones during my act, do I?'

'I don't think you should be ashamed of being a butler,' said Rose, nibbling at the tail of her gingerbread cat. 'But I do think you are using a trapdoor.'

'Ha!' said Dodge. 'The trapdoor under the stage goes nowhere at all.'

'Yes it does. To the Stairs Below.'

The Master of Mysteries spat tea all over the floor.

'All right, who's been spying?' he demanded hotly. 'Are you working for one of my rivals? When I catch the rogue who's behind it—'

'No, no!' cried Rose. 'I'm not a spy. But I do know you're Harry Dodge, and you once studied at the Hall. If there is a door to the Stairs Below under the stage, known only to you, all you need is a trapdoor under your magical box. Once you're under the stage, you can run beneath the theatre, out another secret door and come back for your grand entrance. Using the Infinity Key you keep in that box.' Rose pointed to the key in the trick box she had opened. 'Isn't that how you did it?'

The young man looked flabbergasted. Emily stared open-mouthed at Rose.

'Did one of the butlers watch the act?' demanded

Dodge. 'Blasted Silvercrest Hall! Wasn't it enough that they chucked me out?'

'I don't know if any butlers have,' said Rose. 'But I've taken an interest in the Hall and the butler murders. Argyle – my butler – was a victim.'

'Oh,' said Harry Dodge faintly. 'I see.'

Emily looked dismayed. 'There was no interference from the Netherworld?'

'Only in a manner of speaking,' said Dodge, with a weak smile. 'After all . . . the Stairs Below . . . one can't always be in touch with the Other Side, Miss Proops. It's a bit unreliable.'

Emily nodded bracingly. 'Oh yes. I quite understand.'

Rose leaned forward. 'You don't disappear from the stage all that long, Mr Dodge. It's not long enough for you to have run all the way to my house and murdered Argyle.'

'Well, I should hope not!' said Dodge, sounding shocked. 'As if I'd murder someone!'

'It's just that you have an Infinity Key,' Rose

explained. 'And you did get expelled from Silvercrest Hall.'

'Yes, I did. But my goodness, Miss Raventhorpe, I was glad to leave the place! Far too stuffy and formal for me. I'm much better off living my life on the stage.'

Rose eyed him keenly. Was he telling the truth? Dodge certainly looked and sounded genuine. Emily seemed to have no doubts.

'Oh, you would be wasted as a butler, Mr Dodge!' she exclaimed, waving her black fan. 'I have a butler named Spillwell, and he's very loyal, but dreadfully severe. It is not a situation that suits everyone.'

'Who do you think has murdered the butlers, Mr Dodge?' Rose asked.

'Oh, if anyone is a likely murderer it's the Crows,' said Dodge. 'They've always hated the Silvercrest Hall butlers. I can see Lizzie Deacon stabbing someone. She's good with a sword, and they'd do anything to get rid of the Guardians.'

'But your act is named the Bodysnatch Trick,' said Rose. 'Why call it that, if you don't like the Crows?'

'It's dramatic!' said Dodge, and Emily nodded vigorously. 'Dark, and theatrical, you know.'

'I suppose so,' said Rose. 'But it might be a good idea to stop using the Stairs for a while.'

'What?' Dodge exclaimed. 'Why?'

'Because the Black Glove murderer has an Infinity Key,' Rose told him. 'We saw him in the Stairs Below, after Herrick the beggar was murdered.'

'Herrick was murdered?' exclaimed Dodge. 'The old beggar?'

'Yes, he was. So Miss Regemont has banned the butlers from using the Stairs.'

'Oh dear,' said Dodge, turning pale. 'But my act – it's terribly popular. I can't just drop it. I simply can't.'

'Please don't risk your life, Mr Dodge,' begged Emily. 'I couldn't bear it if the murderer stabbed you. The theatre world would lose a brilliant star.'

'Well – if you insist, Miss Proops.' Dodge seemed to assume a noble attitude. 'I shall avoid the use of my Infinity Key in the Stairs Below. You will let me know when the murderer is caught, won't you?' Dodge looked a little uneasy.

'Yes,' said Rose. 'We promise.' She stood up. 'Thank you very much for talking to us, Mr Dodge, but we'd better go. We did enjoy your act.'

'It was a work of genius,' said Emily. Dodge took her gloved hand and kissed it gallantly. 'Glad you both liked it. Beats the other acts, I can tell you! And er – if you could keep the secret about my act to yourself, I'd be much obliged.'

'I might have to tell Heddsworth,' said Rose.

'Oh well. He's discreet,' said Harry Dodge, not looking fully convinced. 'He knows a lot about the Stairs Below. I hope he never takes up a career as an escapologist, or I'll have serious competition!'

*

Back in the Proops carriage, Emily chattered. 'Wasn't he superb? We can rule him out as a suspect, can't we?'

'Perhaps,' said Rose. 'Or perhaps he's a better actor than he seems.'

'I love his voice,' sighed Emily. 'Imagine how he would sound reading poetry. At any rate, it was lovely to have an evening out. We should go again to that theatre – without worrying about, you know, butlers and such. Too much of that sort of thing,' she added, with a wave of her jet-black handkerchief, 'is bad for the constitu—'

Something flew through the open carriage window, into Rose's lap. A cold, limp, furry thing.

A dead black cat.

Emily screamed. Rose's hands shook. Nausea churned in her stomach.

The carriage jerked to a halt. Their driver flung open the carriage door, grabbed the corpse and threw it into the gutter.

'Saw some cloaked fellow run up and hurl it in,'

he growled. 'Tried to cut him with the whip, but he scarpered. You all right, misses? Nasty shock it must have been.'

'We're fine,' Rose managed to say. 'Just a prank. A nasty prank.'

'We must take you home.' Emily hugged Rose. 'Here, try my smelling salts.' She glared out at the Clarion. 'Horrible place. See if we come here again!'

Chapter 9

The Doctor of Dissection

Shaken as she was by the experience outside the Clarion, Rose was determined to carry on with her investigation. The next morning she talked Emily into returning to the Shudders.

'Herrick was stabbed in broad daylight,' she explained to her friend, as they arrived at the scene of the murder. 'So it's possible there was a witness to the crime. We're right across the road from the medical school.'

Emily pulled her black cloak closely around

her shoulders. 'How thrilling!' she breathed. 'Are we going to ask them straight out if they saw the murder?'

'We'll see,' said Rose. She had dressed again in her oldest clothes, not wanting to be identified as Lord Raventhorpe's daughter. 'It would be useful to talk to Dr Jankers, but also to his butler. I don't know anything about him, but he could be very useful. We just have to find out if he saw anything when Herrick was killed.'

'Oh, this will be fun!' said Emily. 'I've heard that people call Dr Jankers the Doctor of Dissection. I expect it's done by candlelight on stormy nights, and there are gruesome experiments.'

They hesitated on the doorstep. The building looked forbiddingly grim, especially in the chill of early morning. The window display included bottles of murky syrup, pickled rats, boxes of dried lizards and old-fashioned medical tools. A massive syringe rested in a velvet case.

Rose rapped on the door and waited. She glanced at the windows, looking for the butler.

'Hello?' chirped a voice.

A shabbily dressed man had opened the door. His cheeks bunched like apples as he smiled. His gloved fingers twitched on the doorknob. Shy, bird-bright eyes met hers.

'Can I help you, young ladies?'

'Er – we were looking for Dr Jankers,' Rose said.

She noticed the butler peering up and down the street, as if sword-wielding murderers were lurking out of sight.

'I'm afraid the doctor is extremely busy. Is it an urgent matter?'

'Yes, please,' said Emily, with her most charming smile. 'We require some Necrodrops.'

The man nodded – and smiled. 'Ah, those Necrodrops are wonderfully popular! But we are rather short at the moment.'

'That's all right, Mr. . . ?' prompted Rose.

'Lorimer. I'm the butler.'

'Thank you, Lorimer,' said Rose brightly. 'We'll wait inside.'

He looked anxious. 'Inside? Well – the doctor doesn't like being interrupted in his work.'

'We won't bother the doctor at all, sir,' said Emily.

'I suppose not. If it's only some Necrodrops . . . would you step this way?'

The girls followed him down a passageway and into a laboratory. Rose drank in every detail, filing items away in her memory. There was an overpowering smell of camphor, combined with the odours of plasters, pills, lotions, tinctures, syrups and oils. In the middle of the room stood a man weighing blue powder on a set of scales. Enormous, gingery sideburns dwarfed the spectacles perched on his sharp nose.

'Yes?' he said, without looking around.

'Excuse me, Dr Jankers, these young ladies require some Necrodrops.'

The doctor grunted. 'Good Lord, Lorimer, must you bring every customer in here? This is not a chemist shop.'

'Oh no, sir. Rather breezy outside, sir. Didn't want the young ladies catching a chill.'

'They'll have to wait.' The doctor snapped his fingers. 'I need the ingredients for the catarrh preparation.'

Lorimer leapt into action. He arranged bottles, measured and poured. His master barked out orders. 'Careful – I'm sure it was five drops of that particular tincture.'

'Three, I believe, sir,' murmured Lorimer apologetically.

'Of course, of course!'

The butler added the ingredients to the catarrh mixture with skill and care. The doctor fussed and fumed over each addition, muttering about the terrible cost of ingredients nowadays, and their poor quality. Wisps of smoke rose from the crucibles. Rose wondered at Lorimer's patience.

'I think you'll find the preparation is ready now, sir.'

'I knew that. Move aside.' The doctor poured a smoking blue liquid into a bottle. 'Now, the Necrodrops ... Damn, we're out of labels. I suppose I'll have to fetch them myself! Get busy and clean up.'

His butler did not even blink at the doctor's rudeness. Rose felt indignant on Lorimer's behalf. She was tempted to say something about it, but the doctor disappeared down the passageway.

'He can be hasty, I'm afraid,' said Lorimer. 'But he is a great man. He lives for scientific discoveries.'

'Very – noble,' said Rose.

'I dare say there is great pressure on him as a medical man,' agreed Emily.

'Oh, there is, miss! And we had that trouble in the street yesterday, which he fears will be bad for business. You see, a beggar was stabbed to death. Killed on the spot.'

'Oh!' Rose exclaimed, pretending to be shocked. 'How awful!' She paused. 'Did you see it happen?' She watched his face carefully.

He shook his head. 'No, I was making up preparations with the doctor.' The butler's fingers trembled a moment as he picked up a bottle of green liquid. 'The beggar wasn't always a – well, it was a sad way for the man to go.'

'Why do you suppose anyone would kill a beggar?' Rose asked him. As she chatted to the butler, Emily discreetly wandered around the laboratory, peering at the labelled bottles.

'Oh – I suppose it could be for anything,' said Lorimer. 'Perhaps he quarrelled with someone.'

'Perhaps he had something important on him,' said Rose. 'Something worth stealing.'

Lorimer blanched. 'I – I hardly think so.' His fingers went to his throat, fiddling with a fine silver chain. Rose shot a look at her friend.

'It's all very distressing. I am a butler, and there seems to be someone—' he gulped, and dabbed his forehead with a handkerchief. 'Someone murdering them all.'

'That is frightening,' said Rose. 'Have you talked to anyone about it? Any friends?'

The butler shook his head violently.

'No! It's too distressing. I would much rather help the doctor in his work.'

'But what if you knew something that could help to catch the murderer?' asked Rose.

He cast a haunted look at her. 'I . . . I do hope the murderer is found. Very soon. I am not a brave character, or a good fighter, and if the murderer decided to kill me . . . '

He was twisting his hands together. Emily took out her smelling salts, ready to apply them to his nose if he grew faint. Rose concentrated on Lorimer.

'Yes?' she prompted.

'Well . . . shortly after the stabbing . . . I—'

At that moment Dr Jankers returned, scowling. 'That storeroom is a disaster, Lorimer. You are to clean it up properly as soon as you've made this morning's deliveries. And I need to see about getting new cadavers for dissection. There's a shocking shortage from the prisons, nobody seems to bother with executions any more. Now, young lady . . .' He looked Rose in the eye, and seemed a little surprised by the cool way she looked back. *Fancy talking like that about executions*, Rose thought.

He handed the girls a tiny bottle of Necrodrops each. 'That's our last batch. I'll have to charge double for the inconvenience.'

Rose took an embroidered purse from her pocket and shook out the coins. 'We were just talking, Dr Jankers, of that poor beggar who was murdered.'

'Hmm? Oh, that,' said the doctor. 'No great loss, is it? Another useless creature off the streets.'

Rose glared at him. Emily capped her smelling salts with a loud, disapproving click. Lorimer looked embarrassed.

'He deserves a decent burial, at least,' said Rose. 'Unless the Crows – the grave-robbers – get to him first.'

Dr Jankers snorted. 'I don't condone grave-robbery – a repulsive business – but a body used for medical science is at least of benefit to the world. It's a nuisance that there aren't enough bodies for it. My medical school needs them if we are to make any kind of profit. Now Lorimer, you have those deliveries to make. Hurry up. You've taken too long with errands of late. Sheer laziness.'

'Of course sir. Directly! Directly!'

'We'll go out with you,' said Rose quickly. 'Thank you, Dr Jankers. By the way, did you see anything when that beggar was murdered?'

The doctor flicked a suspicious glance at her. 'I did not. Lorimer's all worked up about it, but I don't see why.'

'There have been a number of butlers murdered lately,' Rose pointed out.

'Aren't those to do with burglaries? There's no

diamonds or gold here. Goodbye, and thank you for your custom.'

The doctor's comments about cadavers made Rose uneasy. She wondered what lengths he would go to if he desperately wanted a corpse to dissect.

Emily pushed a piece of paper into Rose's hands. Rose scanned it. It was an article torn from a medical journal.

The esteemed Dr Jankers of Yorke Medical School hosted a dissection for the benefit of a dozen medical students last Tuesday evening. It was an edifying event, and the doctor spoke on the nervous system. Dr Jankers is well known for his creation of Necrodrops, which are an effective sleeping draught.

'Look at the date!' whispered Emily. 'That dissection was only last week. He's getting bodies from somewhere.'

'Ha!' breathed Rose. So Dr Jankers could be in league with the Crows! He could have orchestrated the murders of the butlers, to keep them from patrolling in the graveyard.

She looked sharply at Lorimer. He seemed anxious and fidgety in Dr Jankers' presence.

Rose scrabbled in her pocket for paper and a pencil, and wrote a quick note.

Mr Lorimer, please meet us at Silvercrest Hall tonight. We must discuss the matter of the butler murders. R. Raventhorpe.

Sidling up to Lorimer, Rose slipped the note into his gloved hand. He started. Then, with a nervous glance at Dr Jankers, he opened it.

'Lorimer, would you get on with those deliveries!' barked Dr Jankers.

Lorimer jumped, pocketed the note, and scooped up a pile of packages. 'Goodbye, young ladies,' he mumbled over the top, and was gone.

Chapter 10

Poison and Plots

'Dr Jankers in league with the Crows?' Miss Regemont raised her eyebrows. 'You really think that possible, Miss Raventhorpe?'

Rose sat in Miss Regemont's study. As soon as she had delivered Emily safely home, Rose had gone straight to Silvercrest Hall to discuss their findings. Her butler friends gazed at her in consternation. 'Good heavens,' said Heddsworth at last. 'We sent you to visit Mr Dodge, and you come back with accusations against Dr Jankers?'

'I've told you, I think Dodge is innocent,' said Rose. 'He couldn't have committed those murders. He didn't have time. But Dr Jankers needs bodies to dissect, and the Crows must supply them to someone.' She showed them the piece of paper from the School.

'Suspicious,' Bronson muttered.

'Did you have any luck finding the Crows?' Rose asked them.

'We searched the Muckyards,' said Charlie Malone. 'But . . . A cunning lot, the Crows.'

'Maybe they were near the theatre,' Rose suggested. 'Someone threw a dead cat at me.'

'What?' chorused her listeners.

'Through the carriage window,' said Rose. 'I didn't see who did it.'

There was a shocked silence.

'I shall ring for Arundel. He is here having tea,' said Miss Regemont, going to a bell-pull on the wall. 'He is the Archbishop's butler, and the Archbishop sometimes has news of use to us.

Perhaps he has heard of Dr Jankers' doings.'

The door opened, and Arundel came in. He was a white-haired, scholarly looking butler, who smiled at the assembled company.

'Arundel,' said Miss Regemont. 'Do sit down. Have you any news that may help us? It seems that Dr Jankers, of the medical school, may be in league with the Crows.'

Arundel's brow wrinkled. 'Dr Jankers?' he said vaguely. 'Oh! Yes, I am afraid certain rumours have reached the Archbishop. But the Archbishop refused to credit them. It would be a dreadful scandal if he was proved to be working with bodysnatchers.'

'It would indeed, and I hope the rumours are false. Lorimer is coming tonight to talk to us,' said Miss Regemont. 'Miss Raventhorpe thinks he may know something.'

'Lorimer?' said Arundel, sounding surprised. 'Well, that would help. The Archbishop is deeply concerned about the murders. He even warned me to be on my guard. I assured him that I would be fully prepared to repel an attack.'

Charlie Malone's dancing eyes met Rose's. She stifled a smile. It was hard to imagine this elderly man fighting off anything stronger than a puppy.

'Are you sure Lorimer is coming, Miss Raventhorpe?' inquired Miss Regemont. 'It is getting rather late.'

'I'm sure he will,' said Rose, but she felt uncomfortable. Perhaps Lorimer had not worked up the nerve to come. Or Dr Jankers had prevented him.

Suddenly Lorimer stumbled through the door.

At first, Rose thought he was drunk. He looked dishevelled, pale and ill. He wheezed and choked. Veins bulged in his neck. Something – a tin – clattered from his hand to the floor. Rose leapt up and seized his arm. 'What's happened? What is it?'

He leaned towards her, gasping. He tried to speak. Then he collapsed, unconscious, at her feet.

*

Lorimer's life was only saved by Heddsworth's quick action. He instantly produced a medical kit, containing volatile salts, brandy, safety pins, a thermometer, cough drops, scissors, tweezers, a hot-water bottle, mint-flavoured mouthwash and various antidotes. Thanks to his treatment, Lorimer was now recovering in a Hall dormitory. A burly butler guarded his room.

Miss Regemont had found the tin Lorimer had dropped, and it now sat on her desk. Rose and her friends stared at it.

'Poisoned silver polish,' Miss Regemont said grimly. 'Absorbed through his skin.'

'Poison!' said Bronson, pale with shock. 'Jankers poisoned him to stop him from talking?'

Rose was astonished. 'Why didn't Dr Jankers stab him to death, like the others?'

'It would be harder to trace,' said Bronson darkly. 'The fiend!'

'This doesn't make him the Black Glove murderer,' warned Heddsworth. 'We don't know for certain that it was Jankers who did the poisoning.'

'But who else would? He's the Doctor of Dissections, all right,' said Charlie Malone in disgust. 'I only wish we could arrest him ourselves.'

'Innocent or guilty, you must confront him,' Miss Regemont declared. 'Miss Raventhorpe, will you come back here tomorrow morning? Heddsworth, Bronson and Mr Malone will go with you.'

'Yes, I'll tell Mother I'm shopping,' said Rose eagerly.

'Very good. Lorimer is still too weak to talk, but by tomorrow he should be well enough,' said Miss Regemont. 'This time the murderer has failed to kill his victim. If Dr Jankers is guilty, this may be the proof we need to convict him.'

The next morning, Rose knocked on the gloomy door of the medical school.

Emily stood at her side, eager to see a dramatic confession. The butlers were all armed. And

Lorimer was with them – very peaky about the face, but almost himself again. 'I'm sure it wasn't Dr Jankers,' he kept saying unhappily. 'He would never be in league with bodysnatchers!'

'You were poisoned, Lorimer,' chided Bronson. 'With silver polish. Let us speak to the doctor, and let him explain himself.'

Lorimer glanced nervously at Bronson's rapier. It seemed doubtful that Bronson would permit much explaining.

'It's all right, Lorimer,' said Charlie Malone. 'We won't let Jankers harm you.'

Rose fiddled with her cameo. Dr Jankers must be the murderer! Lorimer didn't want to admit the truth, but he must see that the man was dangerous.

They heard footsteps. The door slowly opened.

'What is this?' said Dr Jankers, staring at visitors. He saw his butler, and scowled. 'And where have you been, Lorimer? Off wasting time? This will come out of your wages!'

Lorimer gulped. 'Sir . . . these are friends of mine, and they wish to speak to you about . . . well . . .'

'Lorimer was poisoned yesterday,' said Heddsworth. 'With silver polish. May we come in and speak to you about it?'

Dr Jankers looked flabbergasted. Rose and her friends walked down the hallway to the laboratory.

It was strewn with spilled powders and upturned bottles. Burners smoked. Broken scales swung tipsily.

'Oh, sir!' sighed Lorimer.

'What a mess!' said Charlie Malone.

'Is it always like this?' Bronson asked, gingerly stepping around a puddle of orange bubbles.

'Only when Lorimer isn't here to help,' said Rose, earning a glare from Dr Jankers.

'What is this nonsense about poisoning?' he demanded.

'Lorimer came to visit us last night, and nearly died from a smear of silver polish,' snapped Bronson.

'Which he must have used before he came to Silvercrest Hall,' put in Charlie Malone. 'Didn't you, Lorimer?'

'I – well – yes,' stammered Lorimer.

'You poisoned him, didn't you?' cried Bronson, pointing at the doctor.

Dr Jankers gasped in outrage. 'How dare you, madam! Outrageous!'

'I'm sure he didn't mean to,' protested Lorimer feebly.

Rose turned to a pile of jars and tins on the nearby bench.

'You make silver polish, don't you, Dr Jankers?'

Dr Jankers gaped at her. He actually looked flustered behind his spectacles. 'Yes – of course – it's a saleable product.'

'But Lorimer usually makes it, doesn't he? Because he makes nearly everything you sell.'

'I beg your pardon!'

Lorimer made frantic silencing gestures at Rose. She ignored him.

'And he was poisoned by a smear of polish,' Rose continued. 'I think Lorimer used a batch of polish *you* made, Dr Jankers.'

Lorimer covered his face with his hands.

'Which was so poisonous it nearly killed him.'

Dr Jankers gasped. 'I made a perfectly good batch, I assure you!'

'I'm afraid it wasn't, sir,' said Lorimer unhappily. 'I fear you miscalculated the ingredients. We must not sell those tins to anyone. They must be destroyed at once.'

'What?' Dr Jankers looked outraged.

'It was accidental,' pleaded Lorimer, to Rose and her friends. 'You must see that.'

Rose looked pointedly at the dishevelled laboratory. 'He doesn't do very well without you.'

'He's been dodging work,' snapped the doctor. 'Only just come back from his little holiday.'

'You should show him some loyalty,' Rose fired

back. 'Because Lorimer is loyal to you. He would rather claim the Black Glove murderer was behind his poisoning than you.'

'You impertinent chit!'

'You know it's true – don't you, Lorimer?'

Lorimer's miserable expression told her the truth. 'Anyone can make a mistake,' he pleaded to Rose. 'Dr Jankers is under great pressure – he never meant me harm!'

Dr Jankers was silenced at last. The silence was punctuated by small explosions from the laboratory burners.

'I – well.' The doctor coughed. 'It is – within the realm of possibility – that I made a small miscalculation.'

'A miscalculation!' said Charlie Malone hotly. 'Lorimer almost died!'

The doctor looked aghast. 'But I didn't mean to do him any harm. I meant to make the silver polish good and strong.'

'Fatally so, I'm afraid,' said Heddsworth.

'So he's innocent?' Bronson sounded disappointed.

'Ah. Well.' Dr Jankers cleared his throat. 'There's no need to go talking of this, is there?'

Rose folded her arms.

'If you let Lorimer make up all the medicines,' she said, 'and treat him decently—'

'Of course he will!' said Lorimer. Rose shook her head at him.

'I suppose,' Jankers muttered, 'that it would be more convenient if he made up the medicinals. I would have more time for important research.'

'Your research?' said Rose. 'Oh yes – the dissections. Emily found an article about your special dissection evenings. They're popular, aren't they? But you must want a regular number of corpses to work on. Where do you get them from?'

'I've told you before, miss, that I use legal sources. I deplore and abhor the practices of bodysnatchers!'

'He does indeed,' said Lorimer eagerly. 'We have a young man who organises a purchase when there is a fresh corpse at the prison. A respectable medical student.'

Rose paused. 'A student who visits the prison, and arranges to buy bodies? You pay him?'

Dr Jankers glared back at her over his spectacles. 'We do, miss – it's only right to give the boy some help. Students don't always have well-lined pockets, you know. He's a useful lad – good at obtaining rare ingredients, things I need, and cheaply . . . '

Rose frowned. 'What is his name?'

The doctor waved a hand. 'Morgan, Morton – something like that.'

'He's a quiet chap,' explained Lorimer. 'Not the friendliest sort, but I don't see much of him.'

Rose turned to Lorimer. 'Do you know much of the Crows, Lorimer? Have you met any of them?'

'Oh, I never patrol in the graveyard!' Lorimer

flinched at the prospect. 'I am glad not to have a proper acquaintance with those creatures.'

'Ah,' said Heddsworth.

'What?' snapped the doctor.

'I'm afraid you may be dealing with a young man named Mortloyd,' said Heddsworth. 'He is, in fact, a Crow. A bodysnatcher.'

Rose actually began to feel sorry for Dr Jankers. His face turned purple.

'Mortloyd! Are you saying I was taken in by a – that I've been using – bodysnatchers!' He sat down heavily. 'My career will be ruined!'

Rose played with her cameo, thinking. Dr Jankers seemed utterly genuine in his shock and remorse.

'I'm sorry, but it's true,' she said. 'We thought you were in league with the Crows, and were murdering the butlers of Yorke.'

'Oh, charming,' grumbled the doctor. 'I've done no such thing. Tell them, Lorimer!'

'It's true,' said Lorimer earnestly. 'I was working

with the doctor when the murders have occurred. Some evenings we have been attending lectures on new scientific developments, with dozens of other witnesses. I assure you he has an alibi.'

'Oh,' said Bronson, disgruntled. 'So . . . the Crows are the most likely suspects after all.'

'You mean the bodysnatchers have been murdering those butlers?' demanded Dr Jankers. 'As well as deceiving me? I will do anything I can to bring them down. Especially Mortloyd. Damnable imp.'

'That would be very helpful, sir. Thank you,' said Heddsworth.

Rose turned to Lorimer. 'But Lorimer – you came to Silvercrest Hall after I gave you that note. If you weren't coming to give evidence against Dr Jankers, what were you going to tell us?'

Lorimer blushed as every eye focused on him.

'Well, Miss Raventhorpe, you asked if we saw anything suspicious when poor Herrick was murdered. I – I'm afraid I did see something. Not the actual stabbing, mind you. But I did see Mr Harry Dodge standing near the body.'

'Harry Dodge?' gasped Bronson. Emily dropped her fan.

'Wait a minute,' Charlie spluttered. 'How could Harry Dodge have murdered Herrick? This doesn't make any sense!'

Rose swallowed her own shock, and thought fast. 'When we spoke to Dodge, he said . . . he spoke as if he'd never heard of Herrick being killed.'

'But Miss Raventhorpe, didn't you say Dodge had an alibi for the murders?' asked Heddsworth.

'Yes,' said Rose slowly. 'He was onstage at those times. And although he uses the Stairs Below in his vanishing act, it wasn't possible for him to have committed those murders before he reappeared. There wasn't enough time.'

'Oh no,' said Emily. 'Since we met Dodge, I've collected clippings on him.' She dug a small scrapbook out of her skirt pocket. To the amazement of everyone in the room, she turned the pages to show articles cut from newspapers and theatrical papers. 'He cancelled his act for a whole week. About the time of the murders, I believe. There were all sorts of speculations as to why. That he was ill, or that he had travelled to the Netherworld . . . it was all tremendously fascinating.'

Rose could hardly believe her ears.

'Emily! How could you not have told me? This makes Dodge a suspect.'

'A leading suspect,' agreed Bronson. She laid her hand on her rapier hilt. 'If he turns out to be a back-stabbing traitor . . .'

'But he's innocent,' Emily protested. 'He would never hurt anyone. Really, you mustn't jump to conclusions.'

'We must speak to Dodge again this afternoon,' said Rose firmly. 'At once. I think it best we meet with him alone – just myself and Emily.'

'I know where he lives,' said Emily, hugging her scrapbook and blushing. 'I know his address.'

'Go to his lodgings? The home of a potential murderer?' said Bronson.

'We will be careful!' said Rose.

'I know you will,' said Heddsworth soberly. 'But we will be outside while you talk to him. Take care, Miss Raventhorpe.'

'He's not a murderer,' said Emily crossly. 'You'll see. He has the soul of an artist. He is not the Black Glove.'

'Well, somebody is,' said Rose. *And if Dodge killed Argyle*, she added to herself, *I will make sure he never escapes from anything again.*

Chapter 11

The Mysterious Mr Dodge

Rose's carriage bumped over the cobblestones. The weather had turned chilly. Wine-red leaves turned muddy underfoot. The sky was the colour of dirty dishrags, and Yorke's streets were thick with fog. Puddles splashed under the carriage wheels, and potholes had turned into quagmires. Gargoyles clung to the cathedral's roof with icy claws. Even its carved saints looked out of sorts. Emily looked out of sorts herself, holding her scrapbook to her like a shield. Rose hoped she would not be too upset if Dodge proved to be guilty.

Dodge lived in a down-at-heel part of Vicarsgate. When they arrived, Emily knocked on the door. Dodge himself opened it.

'Miss Proops!' said Dodge delightedly. 'And Miss Raventhorpe! What an honour. A personal visit! Welcome to my humble abode.'

They entered a small dark parlour, which smelled of damp. Dodge settled the girls in moth-eaten armchairs, and provided cups of tea and Yorke buns. While he put the tea-tray together with butler-like efficiency, Rose looked around the room. She liked the models of hot-air balloons, and the rows of books above the fireplace. They had titles like *Gothic Poetry – Fifty Odes to Wondrous Woe*; *Circus and Zoo Management*; and *Splendiferous Bangs – the Conjuror's Stock in Trade.*

'Mr Dodge,' Rose began, 'we happen to know

you were talking to Herrick the beggar the day he was stabbed.'

'Oh,' said Dodge. He coughed. 'Really? It must have slipped my mind. I did give him a coin or two sometimes. Felt rather sorry for the chap.'

Rose twirled her cameo in her fingers. 'Is there any chance that you knew Herrick had an Infinity Key? Because it went missing after his death.'

The magician paled. 'Yes, but surely you don't think I killed him? I wouldn't dream of such a thing!'

'Of course you wouldn't,' said Emily, with an indignant look for Rose.

'But his key went missing soon afterwards – and as it turns out, you don't have an alibi for the murders. You cancelled your performances.' She took Emily's scrapbook from under her arm and brandished it in his face. 'You see? Reports from the newspapers!'

'Yes, yes, but I wasn't killing anyone!' Dodge

pushed his hands through his hair. 'I was sick that week. I spent those nights at home, reading Gothic poetry!'

'Can you prove that?' Rose demanded.

'No, but it's the truth,' pleaded Dodge. 'Well . . . mostly.'

'You weren't ill?' Emily paled. 'You're not dying, are you?'

He seemed reluctant to meet her eye. 'No,' he said.

Emily stared at him. 'Then you did something you're not proud of,' she said slowly. 'Mr Dodge, please remember that people have been murdered, and more might be, and it is your duty as an honourable man of Yorke to tell the truth!'

Dodge sat silent for a while. He was evidently struggling with his conscience.

'I would hate to lose your regard, Miss Proops,' he muttered.

'We all do things we're ashamed of,' Emily assured him. 'But you must tell us the truth!'

'Very well,' said Dodge, with a sudden heroic air. 'Let the truth be told. Let me be exposed for my faults and weaknesses. I may be the Master of Mysteries, but I am only human!'

'Yes?' said Rose, a trifle impatiently.

Dodge stood up, as if making a speech onstage. 'I used my Infinity Key in my act. I saw my chance to use it! For the sake of a great performance! For the thrill of the audience! But then—' His voice dropped dramatically. Dodge was once again the Master of Mysteries. 'A dreadful thing happened. One night, after my act, I lost the key.'

'No!' cried Emily.

'It was a terrible moment. I dropped it, and the key disappeared down a drain. Lost for ever. My act was doomed. I had to cancel my performances. I was devastated.'

'But Herrick had a key . . . ' said Rose.

'I never would have taken it from the man,' swore Dodge, 'if he had not died so tragically.

The poor man's spirit had departed. Should I leave his key to fall into his grave with him? To be stolen by some base criminal? No! I took it from his unhappy corpse, and to my deepest shame . . .' He tightened his trembling lips. 'I robbed the dead. I am lower than a worm. To restore your faith in me, I will do the meanest, most paltry of tasks . . .'

'Bravo!' cried Emily. She took a lily from a vase and tossed it at Dodge. 'Oh, bravo sir! Manfully declaimed!'

'I wonder where that cream feather came from, that I found where Herrick was killed,' mused Rose. 'I thought it belonged to Miss Deacon, the Crow.'

Dodge looked perplexed. Then he patted his pockets and drew out a snowy feather. 'Oh, it must have been one of these! A dove feather. I use doves in my magician's act, you see.'

'Of course!' said Rose. 'That explains it! Well,

I can't think of a paltry task for you to do right now, Mr Dodge, but we still can't prove that you didn't commit those murders. We have only your word for it.'

'Oh,' said Dodge, crestfallen. 'Then what can I do?'

'Turn yourself in,' said Rose.

'What?' shrieked Emily.

'I mean to Miss Regemont,' said Rose. 'Tell her what you have told us. Better that than be publicly arrested here by the police on suspicion of murder.'

'Rose, you can't!' Emily protested.

Dodge gulped. However, he resumed his noble attitude. 'No, Miss Proops. I see the wisdom of Miss Raventhorpe's argument. I cannot prove my innocence. I must confess, and fall upon the mercy of the butlers.'

'Thank you,' said Rose in relief. 'It would look very bad, you know, if you ran away to avoid capture.'

For a moment Dodge looked tempted to do just that. 'Yes,' he admitted sadly. 'It would.'

'Then pack a bag with your things. Heddsworth followed us in the Silvercrest Hall carriage, and he should be waiting outside.'

Emily stood in indignation as Dodge went to obey. 'This is too bad of you, Rose!' she exclaimed. 'How can you do this to an innocent man?'

'I'm sorry!' said Rose. 'He does seem innocent, but the evidence is stacked against him.'

She paused. 'But if Dodge lost his key a week ago, anyone could have found it – even one of the Crows.'

'You see?' said Emily triumphantly. 'We only need to prove that the Crows were responsible, and Mr Dodge will be saved from suspicion.'

Dodge reappeared with a bag of clothes. 'Ladies,' he said, with a bow. 'I am sure everything will be cleared up in no time.'

'It will, Mr Dodge,' said Emily fervently. 'We shall do our best to clear your name.'

Dodge sighed. 'If you can find the real killer, young ladies, I'll give you a lifetime's tickets to my performances. I think this murderer is the real Master of Mysteries!'

Chapter 12

Cat in the Cathedral

It was Sunday evening, and the bell-ringers of Yorke were tolling every bell in the city.

Peals rang from the cathedral, from St Mary of the Stars, from the tiny kirk of St Aidan's and the stately St Peter's of the Keys. It was all so serene – and yet another cat statue had gone missing. The charming one on Parksgate of a kitten playing with a butterfly. Rose felt angry, as if someone had kidnapped a real kitten. And she was having bad dreams about the prophecy. Nightmares of thunderous skies, crumbling walls and unquiet ghosts.

In her bedroom, she tightened the velvet bow under her chin. The dead cat thrown at her outside the theatre lingered in her memory. Somebody had threatened her. Somebody didn't want her to find the Black Glove murderer.

Resolutely, she picked up her hymnbook, her purse for alms and her parasol and went downstairs to join her mother in the carriage. Lady Constance had returned from her visit to London with five new dresses and an appointment for another portrait sitting. The portrait was to be titled *The Black Swan at the Piano.* Rose thought it should be called *Lady Constance Showing off her Diamonds.*

The city was thick with fog. The Raventhorpe ladies descended from their carriage and walked serenely into the cathedral for the evening service.

The Archbishop and choir led them in a hymn. Their voices soared up and up, echoing against the stone walls and the overarching roof. Candle flames quivered, adding a soft glow to the magnificence around them.

The service ended with the blessing. Rose put her hymnbook with her mother's on the pew. It always took a while to leave the cathedral, as her mother chatted to friends. While Lady Constance was engaged in conversation, Rose edged towards the back of the cathedral.

She threaded through the crowd, keeping a watchful eye on her mother. Lady Constance was talking to the Archbishop. Then she walked down the nave, past ornate Elizabethan tombs. Few people lingered here. Rose pretended to admire the windows and carvings of the cathedral, while covertly looking around.

She heard the rustle of papers, and spied an open door to what was probably an office. Curiously, she peered in. A man sat at a desk, deeply engrossed in an ancient parchment. The man's attire made her pause. He was dressed as a butler.

Puzzled, she watched him reading. He was thin and white-haired, with a vague, scholarly air. Rose struggled with her memory. Then—

'Arundel!' she exclaimed.

He jumped, and peered at her. 'Yes, miss? Were you looking for me?'

'You're the Archbishop's butler,' Rose remembered. 'We met at Silvercrest Hall.'

'Miss Ravenwood! I mean Raventhorpe! Of course I remember.' He looked down at the parchment. 'I am rather distracted, I'm afraid. Another cat statue missing . . .'

'Yes,' said Rose. 'I know. Have you discovered anything that could help us?'

Arundel looked tired. 'Not at all, Miss Raventhorpe,' he said sadly. 'I fear we are already cursed, with all these murders. The statues are disappearing into thin air, and our protection from Saint Iphigenia will be gone. I hate to think what will happen.' He sighed. 'The very walls of this city owe their strength to the magic of the cats. I've been hunting through Yorke's history, seeking clues as to how to stop this. And there doesn't seem to be anything.'

'Does the Archbishop know about the prophecy?'

'He thinks it a fable,' said Arundel. 'I only wish it was. I must simply carry on in the meantime. Care for the Archbishop's robes, organise his appointments, keep his study in order and see to the general upkeep of the cathedral. Oh, and look after Watchful.'

Rose followed his gaze. Then she blinked in astonishment. A black cat was stalking across the floor.

He sprang up on to a marble tomb and curled up on it. Arundel shook his head. 'I do believe the creature thinks he owns the cathedral.'

'I didn't think animals were allowed in here!' said Rose.

Arundel smiled. 'Watchful is the exception. You might want to look at whose tomb that is.'

Puzzled, Rose went to the cat. He yawned in a lordly manner and permitted her to stroke his ears. She looked at the lid of the tomb, and read:

Here lieth Arlington

steward and manne-at-arms

If e'er the city fair be curst
by terror or by foe,
my Guardians upon the heights
and labyrinths below
will Yorke defend. So churls, beware,
ye are but flesh and bone,
and traitors will imprisoned be
within the walls of stone.

Rose felt a thrill.

'Arlington!' she whispered. 'The Hall founder – he's buried here?'

'Yes, indeed,' said Arundel. 'He was dedicated to the service of Yorke.'

'Is Watchful your cat?'

'No, no, he doesn't belong to anyone. But the Archbishop likes to see him around – says there has always been a cat around the place. Mind you, he makes cleaning the tomb something of a difficulty.' Arundel took a cloth from his pocket and polished the lid around the cat.

Rose noticed another door in the wall: an ancient, oaken door.

He saw her look. 'The door to Ladychurch Tower. I can't go in there. Far too long a climb to the top. My old bones don't permit it any more.'

'May I see it?' asked Rose. 'It must have the most amazing view.'

Arundel scratched his head. 'I'm not sure I have the key.'

Watchful the cat stretched languidly. Then he nudged at Arundel's coat. A set of keys jingled underneath.

'Dear me!' said Arundel absent-mindedly. 'Here they are. Well, perhaps you might go up, Miss Raventhorpe. You are not afraid of heights?'

He produced the ancient key, and unlocked it to reveal spiral steps leading upwards. The wall behind it was panelled wood, but the rest of it was stone.

'One of the oldest parts of the cathedral,' Arundel whispered. 'Some say it was built by Arlington himself. Here you are.' He gave her a candle and matches. Rose lit the candle and put the matches safely in her pocket. 'Go on up. After you've had a look around, we can have a cup of tea. If your mother permits, of course.'

Rose glanced back through the nave. Her mother was still deep in conversation with the Archbishop.

She started up the stairway.

The first flights of steps was easy. After that, Rose slowed down until she was at a steady plod. Just how far up was this tower? Her legs ached, and her lungs felt near to bursting. It took a concentrated effort, and several short rests, to get to the door at the top.

She opened the tower door and stepped out on to the balcony. She blew out the candle and set it down.

A fresh gust of wind took her breath away. Startled birds flew from the stonework. Spread below like a map, as far as she could see, was the city of Yorke.

Argyle had once taken Rose on a moonlight walk around the ramparts of the city walls. To escape Her Ladyship's notice they had climbed out of the window of the butler's pantry. Argyle had carried a burning torch, which made Rose feel as if they had stepped into the medieval past. The sky had blazed with stars. The view was wondrous. But even that experience paled in comparison to this.

The last rays of sunlight broke through a cloud,

illuminating the city in pale gold. The ancient walls encompassed the city. Rose saw the theatres and shops and the Shudders, and the rustling, green glimmer of the park. She saw the River Knoll winding through the city, and the distant, murkier slums known as the Muckyards.

Rose put a hand to her chest. This was her city, the city the Raventhorpes had lived in and fought for over centuries. She was a child of Yorke, and it was under her protection.

Then, down in the street, she saw Emily's butler, Spillwell.

There was no mistaking him, even from such a distance. His tall bony frame, in its severe butler's uniform, and his spectral head, were as recognisable to Rose as her mother's elegant figure.

He entered a skitterway visible from the tower. Rose watched him, breathless.

The butler walked furtively up to a door in a wall. He unlocked the door, stepped inside and closed it behind him. Rose would have bet a thousand pounds that Spillwell had entered the Stairs Below.

She bolted down the tower steps. She gave an incoherent thanks to a startled Arundel – 'Beautiful, lovely, must return to my mother,' – and dashed into the nave.

'There you are, Rose,' Lady Constance exclaimed. 'Goodness, but the Archbishop can talk! Come along, the carriage is waiting.'

'I can't, Mother,' Rose said quickly. 'I know it's getting late, but I promised to stay the night at Emily Proops' house. She's waiting for me outside.'

Lady Constance sighed. 'Really, Rose, you should not make arrangements like that without telling me. Well, don't get run over by a wagon on the way out, or pickpocketed, or anything ghastly.'

Rose managed not to break into a run until she was out of her mother's sight.

Silently, she thanked Argyle for their countless walks around the city. She knew how to take the fastest route, crossing makeshift bridges and ducking down skitterways. It was only when she raced down Spillwell's street that she realised the main impediment.

The door in the wall was locked.

She thumped her head against the door and cursed herself in Latin, Gaelic and Arabic. 'Dolt,' she added in English, for good measure.

Fiddling with her cameo, she thought of rushing back to the cathedral and asking Arundel for his Infinity Key. Then she changed her mind. It would take precious time, and he might insist on coming with her. How could she follow Spillwell now?

Something cracked under her fingertips.

Rose stood frozen, horrified. She had broken her precious cameo!

Quickly she took off the chain. The lovely image of the black cat was unharmed. She opened the locket.

The golden base was loose. Gingerly, Rose pushed it with a fingertip. It flicked upwards, like a tiny door. It was a false base, hiding a secret compartment. And inside the compartment lay a small silver Infinity Key.

Rose stared at it. Her heart beat madly.

She did not doubt that this was Argyle's Infinity Key. She remembered Garnet Goldsmith talking about the locket. She must have created this cameo according to Argyle's instructions.

'Why?' Rose whispered. 'Why did you do it, Argyle?'

Perhaps he had meant to tell her, but died before that was possible. Whatever the reason, she now had an Infinity Key in her hand.

She took the key, and turned back to the door.

The lock clicked. The handle turned. Rose was inside the Stairs Below.

There was no time to waste. She took a lantern from the wall, lighting it with Arundel's matches. Then she locked the door behind her, replaced the key in her locket, and set off into the labyrinth.

The dark tunnels had been unpleasant on her first visit, but then she'd had Heddsworth and his friends with her. Now she was alone in a place she hardly knew. She touched the stone walls as she walked, taking comfort in their solidity. In places she was forced to duck under low-lying stone, or squelch through icy mud. Once a large, whip-tailed rat scurried past her. Rose suppressed a shiver.

The passages began to branch off at random, forcing Rose to choose paths. Each time she found a door, she touched the lanterns on the walls. None of them felt warm, so they couldn't have been used recently. Nor did they contain much oil. She walked on, feeling increasingly anxious.

Think, Rose. You saw Spillwell enter the door near the cathedral. Where would he be going? Hardly towards Silvercrest Hall, when the use of the Stairs is banned. But what if he is the murderer?

He could be going to kill someone. There are grand

houses with butlers in Riversgate. I think I'm heading in that direction . . .

The labyrinth turned and twisted. Rose took path after path, while the lantern-light flickered. She glanced up at the walls, remembering Heddsworth's warning about unsafe passageways. Sudden dread filled her heart. How would she know which sections were unsafe? Were they marked at all? If not – if a tunnel collapsed –

Rose suddenly broke out in a cold sweat.

'So much for being a protector of Yorke,' she scolded herself.

If the worst occurred, nobody would know what had happened to her. *I could be trapped by rockfalls, and run out of air. The rats would gnaw at my bones . . .*

'No,' she said aloud, in a small voice. Then, more loudly, 'No.'

Argyle would be ashamed of her, cringing like this. Her father, Lord Frederick, would be disappointed too. *I thought you wanted adventure, my girl. Raventhorpes don't give up when things get uncomfortable.* Even her mother would have pursed her lips. *Do not whimper, Rose. It is unbecoming in a lady.*

The oil was running low. Her palms grew clammy. She could run back to the last door. But would the light last until then? Surely another would appear soon. If not – if the light went out—

She quickened her pace, heart hammering. She had the nasty feeling she was going in circles. And if she was lost . . . the Infinity Keys were called so for a reason. She could be doomed to wander the Stairs Below for ever.

A door . . . a door . . .

She gave a cry of relief when she found one. It looked decrepit, its timber rotten, but it was still a door. She fumbled for her Infinity Key, and tried the lock. The hinges squealed. She pushed. The door opened a few grudging inches. Then it jammed, stuck tight.

Rose pressed her face desperately to the gap. She smelled whiffs of willow, and the faint tang of the River Knoll. The air was damp with fog. She heard a distant clop of hooves, and rattle of carriage wheels. And voices. Close by. Voices.

'Help!' Rose shouted.

The lantern sputtered, dying. 'No,' she gasped.

Then she felt the trickle of dirt on the back of her neck.

Heddsworth had warned her about old, disused tunnels. The risk they might collapse.

She dropped the useless lantern. 'Help!' she screamed.

Footsteps approached. There were shadows in the fog, hands gripping the edge of the door, heaving it back. Rose pushed her key back into her locket, and leaned all her weight on the door. The hinges creaked and whined. The trickles of dirt fell faster, and a fist-sized rock crashed to the floor. Rose pushed on the door with every last ounce of her strength.

The door jerked open. Rose stumbled through, and the tunnel collapsed behind her with a crash. Dirt and debris filled the air.

Rose gasped for fresh air, hardly able to believe her narrow escape.

'Thank you! I—'

She stopped. Night had fallen outside now, but she knew this place. The tall, mossy stones and statues, the faded inscriptions. The door, she saw, was in a row of ancient vaults.

She was in the graveyard.

And her rescuer . . .

'Well, well, Your Ladyship,' drawled Mortloyd, the youngest of the Crows. 'Back in the graveyard again. Where's your Infinity Key?'

Chapter 13

The Return of Persephone

Lizzie Deacon, Blackthorn and Mortloyd looked like all their Christmases had come at once. They carried spades and lanterns, and had evidently been busy digging up a grave.

'Miss Raventhorpe!' cooed Lizzie. 'All alone?'

'So there's a door to them Stairs here,' said Blackthorn.

'No use without a key,' said Mortloyd.

'Then where's hers?' demanded Blackthorn.

'I don't have one,' Rose lied. 'That door was open already – it's half rotten.'

Lizzie grasped her rapier hilt. 'It would be ungrateful of you, Miss Raventhorpe, to tell us fibs. All we want is one little key. Turn out your pockets!'

Rose stared at them. The Crows didn't have an Infinity Key. They wanted hers.

She wanted to run. To shout defiant words at them. But if she refused to empty her pockets, they would grab her and search her by force. They would steal the locket. They would find the key.

Slowly, Rose complied. She had a few coins and a handkerchief.

Blackthorn scowled. 'Give her a few slices – she'll find it quick enough.'

Lizzie's gaze rested on Rose's cameo. It took all of Rose's self-control not to close her hand around it. Her hands trembled. Lizzie took a step forward.

'Hsst!' said Mortloyd.

Other figures had appeared in the fog. Lizzie

gripped Rose's arm painfully hard, warning her not to cry out. The figures came closer. Rose strained to see them. One was limping, she was sure of it. One was a woman. And the other—

'Miss Raventhorpe?'

Heddsworth emerged from the mist. He, Bronson and Charlie Malone looked sharply from her to the Crows.

'What are you doing here?' Heddsworth asked Rose. 'Are you all right?'

'I—'

'We rescued her from the Stairs Below,' trilled Lizzie Deacon. She pointed towards the vaults. 'A door there! We opened it. Saved her from certain death. Don't we deserve a reward? I know how you butlers feel about debts of honour.'

'Miss Raventhorpe was in the Stairs?' said Heddsworth, startled. Rose's face was on fire.

'I – I was lost,' she admitted. 'The door was jammed – they helped me out. The – the tunnel collapsed.'

After a long moment, Heddsworth nodded, and turned back to the Crows. 'Very well. What do you expect as a reward?'

Lizzie brushed down her skirts. 'Oh, very little. Just the rights to the graveyard. You stop your silly patrolling activities, and let us get on with our business. We'd like to dig up a few bodies in peace for a change.'

The butlers stood dumbfounded.

'You must be mad,' snapped Bronson.

'Now, now,' purred Lizzie. 'Surely Miss Raventhorpe's life is worth it.'

Heddsworth cleared his throat. 'A duel,' he said. 'Single combat. If you win, we give you graveyard rights. If we win, you Crows are forbidden to set foot in here. Indefinitely.'

Rose was horrified. She wanted the other butlers to protest, but they did not bat an eyelash.

Lizzie held a fierce, whispered discussion with her companions. Then she lifted her head, eyes gleaming.

'I don't believe we've had the pleasure of a duel, have we, Heddsworth?'

Bronson stepped forward. 'Not with Heddsworth. You duel with me.'

Annoyance flashed across Lizzie Deacon's features. Then she shrugged. 'If you insist.'

The other two Crows melted into the darkness.

The combatants took the *en garde* position. They began to circle each other, step by measured step.

Lizzie Deacon struck first. Swift as a snake, she whipped her blade across Bronson's cheek. Rose gasped.

But Bronson did not seem daunted by the cut. She skilfully parried Lizzie's next blows, and fought back so ferociously that Lizzie was forced back several paces. The Crow shook back a fallen lock of hair, and took a savage swipe at Bronson. Bronson whirled out of reach, and Lizzie's rapier struck a stone angel so hard its nose flew off.

Infuriated, Lizzie Deacon resumed her attack.

The blades crossed and locked. Blood trickled down Bronson's cheek.

Suddenly, Lizzie lunged forward forcefully, but with the hilt of her rapier. She brought it down on Bronson's wrist with all her force. Bronson gave a gasp of pain, and her rapier fell from her hand. Weaponless, it looked like Bronson would be stabbed through the heart.

Rose could not stand by and see Bronson killed on her behalf. She grabbed the rapier from the ground, and held the blade desperately in both hands. Lizzie's eyes widened with amusement. 'Oh, are we playing a game of lawn tennis? Croquet, perhaps? Go on, Miss Raventhorpe. Single combat. See if you can do better than Miss Bronson.'

Rose had never held a sword, let alone fought with one. But she was a Raventhorpe of Yorke, a protector of the city. And Lizzie Deacon had wanted to dig up Argyle's corpse. With no finesse, but fuelled by rage, she lashed out and caught the edge of Lizzie's wrist.

Lizzie stared down at the scratch as if a kitten had bitten her, and in that second Rose had the rapier to Lizzie's throat, backing her against the angel statue. Her hands shook. What was she supposed to do now?

Heddsworth stepped in, and gently took the rapier from Rose's hands. 'I think you'll find that was a Raventhorpe victory, Miss Deacon.'

Lizzie turned a furious scarlet. She snatched up her weapon, and kicked the stone angel's nose across the grass. 'Keep your dog-poxed graveyard then', she said angrily. 'The Black Glove'll finish you off!'

Rose shuddered before she could stop herself.

Somewhere nearby she heard a curse. Lizzie swept off towards a fresh grave, followed by the butlers and Rose. Mortloyd and Blackthorn had dug down to a coffin – but it was empty.

'What—' began Blackthorn.

'We've been gulled,' cried Lizzie in a rage.

Lantern-lights bobbed towards them. Rose

saw Dr Jankers and several police constables. Dr Jankers' red whiskers trembled with outrage. 'Mortloyd!' he roared. 'You told me those bodies were from reputable sources!'

Mortloyd scowled. 'More fool you,' he muttered.

The police marched forward, brandishing handcuffs. 'You lot are nabbed,' a sergeant said with relish. 'What a nice little gang.'

Lizzie Deacon's lip curled as she turned to the butlers. 'You set a trap!'

'Oh yes,' said Charlie, with a grin. 'I think we staged it all very nicely. A faked funeral, a fancy coffin . . . how could you resist?'

Dr Jankers was still fuming. 'Filthy grave-robbers! Ruining the name of honest research . . . would never have believed it . . .'

'Got you to thank, have we?' Mortloyd stared at Rose. 'Little hoity-toity Miss Raventhorpe?'

'You can keep your spades off this graveyard,' Rose shot back.

The constables had seized and cuffed the Crows. Dr Jankers accompanied them, a picture of indignation. 'I swore to see them clapped in irons!' he declared. 'They dared to ruin the good name of my business!'

Silent and sullen, the Crows left the graveyard in custody. Mortloyd cast a last look at Rose. It felt like a faceful of ice-water.

'Well,' said Charlie cheerfully. 'I think Miss Raventhorpe would like some fencing lessons.'

Bronson sheathed her rapier. 'Indeed,' she said, giving Rose a genuine smile.

'The Crows didn't have an Infinity Key,' said Rose suddenly. 'They wanted mine! So they couldn't have been in the Stairs after Herrick was murdered.'

'Well, there goes another theory,' said Charlie Malone, in some disappointment. 'So they are off our list of suspects.'

Heddsworth took small bottles and bandages from his pockets, and attended to Bronson's hurt wrist and cheek. 'We must disinfect those cuts,' he explained to Rose. 'Cloth in a small fencing injury can kill you if you're not careful. By the way, Miss Raventhorpe, I apologise in advance for saying this, but are you stark, staring mad? I mean, we must thank you for stepping in and fighting. But by Saint Iphigenia and all her cats! You do realise Lizzie could have killed you?'

'I wanted to buy you some time, that's all,' Rose said. 'I wasn't a real threat to her.'

Heddsworth sighed. 'The Raventhorpes,' he muttered. 'Protective to the highest degree. Very well. Tell me this. What were you doing in the Stairs Below?'

Guilt flooded through Rose.

'I – I was following Spillwell. I saw him go through a door after he left the cathedral. Then my lantern ran out of oil . . . '

'You got into the Stairs Below?' said Bronson in astonishment. 'How?'

Rose showed them the cameo with its hidden

base. 'Argyle gave this to me. I didn't know it had a key. It's Argyle's, isn't it?'

'It must be,' said Heddsworth. 'Before he died, Argyle was planning to go overseas with Lord Raventhorpe. He must have thought the key would be safest with you. I suppose he couldn't have guessed you would use it so recklessly!'

'I didn't know I would end up in the graveyard with the Crows!'

'By Grimsgate, Miss Raventhorpe!' Heddsworth paced like a silver-maned lion. 'Key or no key, you took a terrible risk. If you thought Spillwell was acting suspiciously, you should have come to us.'

'There wouldn't have been time!' cried Rose. 'If Spillwell was the murderer, he could have gone after one of you.'

'And if he was, and saw you following him? Miss Raventhorpe, I say this with admiration and even some affection, but you can be mortally stubborn.'

'Better stubborn than – than wishy-washy!' said Rose.

'Ah, it's nothing to be ashamed of,' said Charlie, kindly. 'We're all a bit on the stubborn side.'

Heddsworth was not pacified. 'You know the dangers, Miss Raventhorpe. You saw what happened to Herrick.'

'Of course!' flashed Rose. 'I saw what happened to Argyle, too.'

'All right, enough.' Charlie made a calming gesture. 'Argyle was the one who gave Miss Raventhorpe a key. Clearly he placed a lot of trust in her. And we have encouraged Miss Raventhorpe to help.'

'True,' said Heddsworth. 'But I do want your word that you will not use it again, Miss Raventhorpe, unless in an emergency. Not haring off alone after suspects.'

Rose opened her mouth to protest. Then she thought of Bronson and Lizzie's duel. Bronson could have been mortally injured, and all on Rose's account.

'All right,' she sighed. 'I won't.'

Bronson shook her head. 'So why was Spillwell in the Stairs? Should we really consider him a suspect?'

'Well . . .' began Rose, and stopped. She had no actual proof that Spillwell was up to anything dire.

'Perhaps we should ask him,' suggested Charlie, tidying away bandages. 'After all, he was breaking the ban.'

Heddsworth gazed at Argyle's mortsafe. 'Very well. He might be perfectly innocent, but we must investigate every lead. Especially now the Crows are no longer suspects.'

Rose thought of that scar on Spillwell's wrist. Had he been injured committing an act of murder?

Heddsworth went to the door in the vaults that had led Rose out of the Stairs Below. He forced it shut and locked it with his own Infinity Key. 'Let's go,' he said. 'We must inform Miss Regemont about the arrest of the Crows, and Spillwell's use of the stairs.'

'Miss Raventhorpe, don't tell Miss Regemont about your Infinity Key,' warned Charlie Malone. 'If she finds out that you went into the Stairs Below . . . '

'I won't,' said Rose. She wondered what Miss Regemont would say if she knew Rose had actually fought Lizzie Deacon with a rapier. It would be best not to bring that up, either.

Chapter 14

The Silence of Spillwell

Miss Regemont's crimson skirts rustled. Her shoes tapped the Hall's library floor. Her nostrils flared.

'Spillwell? You now accuse *Spillwell* of being the Black Glove?'

'He was in the Stairs Below,' said Rose. 'I saw him!'

'We must question him, madam,' said Heddsworth. 'The Crows have been arrested, and it seems they did not have a key after all.'

The lady spun on her heel. 'Very well – but another cat statue has gone missing, and Mr Dodge has been secured in a room here at the Hall, with a constant watch on his door. It could not possibly have been Mr Dodge.'

'Oh!' cried Rose in relief. 'Then he's innocent! Emily will be so glad.'

'I will not be so pleased if a butler is our culprit,' said Miss Regemont. 'I sincerely hope that Spillwell can explain himself.'

She went to the wall and rang a service bell. A student butler appeared.

'Be so good as to fetch Spillwell here,' said Miss Regemont. 'Explain to his employer that it is a matter of urgency. We must deal with this matter at once.'

'Consider it done, madam,' said the young man, and left the room.

Heddsworth cleared his throat. 'May I ask if there is any new information on the cat statues' disappearance?'

'Unfortunately not,' sighed Miss Regemont. 'We have heard all sorts of theories. Mr Malone is kept busy writing them all down.'

'Oh yes,' said Charlie, fishing out his notebook. 'Let's see ... "The cats are being stolen by a double agent of the Royal Court, to demoralise the English nation." "The statues are leaving of their own accord, to show the Guardians of Yorke they are failing in their duty." And "the statues are being melted down to make saucepans for Dorabella's teashop."'

Bronson pulled a face. 'Ugh. How—'

'Panicky?' suggested Charlie Malone. 'Well, to be fair, we haven't got any answers ourselves.'

'We must do our best to be calm,' declared Miss Regemont. 'A butler must remain calm in all circumstances. Fetch some polish, please, Heddsworth. While we're waiting we'll clean all the silver in the Hall!'

*

Rose was very tired of silver polish by the time Spillwell appeared in the doorway. He looked his usual cold, spectral self.

'You wished to see me, madam?'

'Ah, Spillwell,' said Miss Regemont. She gestured to an empty chair behind the mountain of teapots and cutlery. 'Do sit down.'

'I would rather not, madam. I understand this is an urgent matter?'

'Quite,' said Miss Regemont. 'I have reason to believe, Spillwell, that you used the Stairs Below today.'

Rose watched Spillwell closely. She hoped to see him look anxious or conscience-stricken.

His face did not change.

'The Stairs Below, madam?'

'You know it is banned. Did you use it, against my orders?'

'I am afraid I was obliged to, madam,' said Spillwell. 'But it is a matter of delicacy, and I will only explain my actions to you in private.'

'Well, really!' said Bronson indignantly.

Miss Regemont lifted her eyebrows at Bronson. 'I understand a butler's need for discretion, thank you Bronson. We shall speak in my study, Spillwell.'

The pair left the room.

'Ugh,' said Bronson. 'I bet he's making up some monstrous fib. He just doesn't want us to hear it.'

'I wish we could duel the truth out of him,' Charlie agreed.

They waited for what felt like forever before Spillwell and Miss Regemont returned.

'Spillwell has explained everything to me,' Miss Regemont said briskly. 'It was not a matter of life and death, but I have heard enough to be satisfied that he meant no harm.'

Spillwell stood beside her, his usual imperturbable self. Rose wanted to kick him. Of course, she did not want Emily's butler to be a murderer, but she still distrusted him thoroughly.

'We aren't to be given any other explanation?' demanded Bronson.

'No, Bronson,' said Miss Regemont firmly.

'I am sorry to have caused any confusion,' said Spillwell, in cold, polite tones. 'May I return to my duties, madam?'

'Yes, Spillwell. You may.'

Spillwell bowed, and left the room. He did not spare the others a glance.

Miss Regemont sighed. 'At least he did not come to harm,' she said. 'If the Black Glove had been in the Stairs Below . . . ' She shook her head. 'As we know another statue has gone . . . Which means we are due for another murder.'

Rose turned things over and over in her mind. It seemed they were back at square one. Anyone could be the murderer. But who else would know about Herrick's past, and the Stairs Below, and the significance of the cat statues?

'If Spillwell is innocent,' she said aloud, 'it could be some other butler, who has been under our noses the whole time.'

Miss Regemont paled at the thought. 'I shall

interview every butler of Silvercrest Hall, starting in the morning. Everyone's movements at the time of the murders must be accounted for. Mr Malone, please inform all the butlers in Yorke that I wish to see them.'

Charlie nodded. 'Very good, madam.'

'Heddsworth, please see Miss Raventhorpe safely home.'

'Could I stay here?' Rose asked. 'Mother thinks I'm staying at my friend Emily's.'

'Oh!' said Miss Regemont, taken aback. 'Yes, that can be arranged. We have guestrooms. Bronson, could you see that Miss Raventhorpe has all she needs? A nightdress, hairbrushes, a bath, some dinner?'

Within an hour Rose was fed, clean, and in bed, in a comfortable room of the Hall. First thing in the morning, she told herself, she would convince Miss Regemont to let her take part in questioning the butlers.

*

Rose was dressing for breakfast when she heard a commotion. With a sense of foreboding, she abandoned her hairbrush and hurried downstairs.

She saw a fuming Miss Regemont, and Bronson and Charlie Malone with their rapiers at the ready. Then she saw Heddsworth, surrounded by police.

'How dare you search Heddsworth's room!' Miss Regemont snapped. 'What possible grounds could you have?'

'Beg your pardon, madam,' said a sergeant, 'but I must ask Mr Heddsworth to accompany me. I am arresting him on suspicion of murder of the butlers Tremayne, Guillaume and Argyle.'

Chapter 15

Chain and Stone

Charlie's jaw dropped. 'What – you're accusing him? *Him*?'

Bronson brandished her rapier. 'This is a disgrace,' she hissed. 'Outrageous!'

'May I ask who has accused me?' Heddsworth calmly inquired.

The sergeant cleared his throat.

'We had an anonymous tip-off. Found some items of interest in your room.'

'Items of interest?' Bronson repeated.

'Black gloves. The same sort as those found with the victims,' said the sergeant. 'And bloodstains on his clothes.'

Bronson, Charlie and Rose burst out in indignation.

'Those aren't his!'

'Someone planted all that in his room – you can't call that evidence!'

'You absolute fools, are you blind?'

The sergeant turned to the butlers.

'If you will kindly hand over your weapons? We don't want a scene in this nice Hall.'

Charlie and Bronson looked all too ready to make a scene. Reluctantly, they gave the sergeant their rapiers. 'You will have them back directly,' the sergeant said, but his eyes narrowed as he inspected the blades.

'Where are you taking him?' demanded Rose.

The sergeant cleared his throat. 'Perhaps someone should escort this young lady home?'

'Don't worry, any of you,' said Heddsworth, as he followed the sergeant out. 'This will all be cleared up, I am sure.'

He stepped into a waiting coach. The sergeant climbed in after him. The other officers climbed aboard, the driver flicked his whip, and the vehicle rolled away.

Bronson stood in the middle of the street. She did not move, even when a wagon nearly knocked her over.

'Saint Iphigenia's cats!' she shouted at last, startling passers-by. 'How could they do it? We should have fought them, Charlie!'

'And get arrested too?' Charlie looked as grim as Rose had ever seen him.

'Heddsworth was framed by a butler, then,' said Miss Regemont. 'Someone who could walk around Silvercrest Hall without anyone thinking it strange. A traitor in our midst! I can hardly believe it!'

'What we need to discover is the motive,' said

Rose. 'We've been side-tracked by the missing Infinity Key, and the Crows, and Dodge and Dr Jankers. *Why* does the murderer want to kill the butlers?'

Her friends looked despairing. Nobody knew.

Rose gripped her cameo so hard it made a red mark on her palm. She, a Raventhorpe, was not going to watch another butler die.

Rose rapped on the door of Yorke Prison.

A former castle, the building still had the crenellated towers, embrasures and arrow slits of medieval defence. Now a prison, it reeked of filth, disease and despair.

She knocked harder, pulling her cloak around her. A hatch in the door slid aside. One fierce, beady eye inspected her. She heard a rude chuckle. Then the bolts were shot, and the massive door creaked open. It revealed a man with a straggling grey beard, yellow teeth and a belly like a greasy barrel. He leered at Rose.

'What're you after, eh, lovey?'

Rose gave him the sharpest of looks. 'I want to see a prisoner.'

'Quality, are we? I can guess who. Cost yer.'

Seething, Rose dropped silver into his grimy palm. He looked her up and down.

'Well, then. Off yer go, and see his 'ighness.' He jerked a thumb towards the far end of the passage.

Tugging her shawl closer, Rose passed the rows of cells. The prisoners leered at her, spat, or whimpered in their misery. Some catcalled, or reached out with fingers like claws. Rose pressed her body against the wall, appalled.

Suddenly a hand shot through the bars, seizing her wrist. With a stifled shriek, Rose pulled away.

'Miss Raventhorpe?' a voice said hoarsely.

Kind, familiar eyes met hers. Rose let out her breath.

'Heddsworth!'

He gave an exasperated sigh. 'How could you

come here, Miss Raventhorpe? And alone! Why not ask Bronson or Mr Malone to escort you?'

Rose was too shocked by Heddsworth's state to listen. He was pale, unshaven and heavy-eyed. His cell contained a tin bucket, a candle-stub and a sorry-looking mattress. The place was bitterly cold.

'Heddsworth, this is horrible! They can't treat you like this!'

'Yes, there is a terrible lack of cutlery,' he said wryly. 'No napkins, no silver, no candlesticks. I shall have to make a formal complaint.'

'I'll bring you some blankets,' said Rose. 'And food.'

'They provide something they describe as food,' said Heddsworth. 'Bronson tried to bring some, but she quarrelled with the guard, and he threw her out. Did you have to bribe him?'

'No,' she lied. 'You mustn't worry, Heddsworth. We'll get you out. Miss Regemont will do everything she can to free you.'

'I know, but if I am convicted . . . ' Heddsworth

stopped himself. 'I have been thinking about Argyle's death, Miss Raventhorpe. Did you know much about his private life?'

Rose knew Argyle had kept secrets from her. But it was still hard to think of him as anything more than butler to the Raventhorpes. She felt uncomfortably aware of her ignorance. Had she truly never asked him about his past? He had always been there, always putting his duties first, telling her stories about the city of Yorke . . .

'No,' she admitted, shamefaced. 'I know he had a brother once. But not much else.'

'I know one of his secrets,' said Heddsworth. 'And it has occurred to me that it could have had a bearing on his death.'

'What secret?'

'He had a love affair,' said Heddsworth. 'With a certain lady.'

'What?'

It was impossible to imagine such a thing of Argyle. At least, not the Argyle she knew. Rose tried to picture him a young man. Going to fencing lessons, strolling around the city, dancing at balls and being charming to young ladies. Could he have fallen in love back then?

Heddsworth sighed. 'He and this lady were very fond of each other. However, they quarrelled, and the affair ended just a short time ago. As his friend I knew about it, and I promised to keep it a secret. Until now.'

'But what would that have to do with his murder?' asked Rose, still reeling from the whole idea of a romance.

'There have been duels among butlers in the past over ladies,' Heddsworth explained. 'I've wondered if the murderer nursed a grudge over something of that nature. If Argyle had beaten a rival for a lady's affections, and his rival was angry enough . . . '

'Perhaps,' said Rose doubtfully. 'But how can you be sure he was in love with the lady? Perhaps they were only friends.'

'Because I know the lady,' said Heddsworth. 'It was Miss Regemont.'

Rose walked to Silvercrest Hall in a daze.

Argyle and Miss Regemont?

Impossible. Impossible!

'Heddsworth imagined it,' she told herself. 'It's a good thing he doesn't gossip. Argyle would have been furious!'

She arrived at the Hall, and explained to the butler at the door that she wished to see Miss Regemont in her study. 'It's just upstairs, I can go myself,' she added.

She would talk to Miss Regemont. She would be calm and courteous. She wouldn't betray Heddsworth's confidence. She would only say that she had heard—

She stopped outside Miss Regemont's door. A familiar swishing sound came from inside the room.

Rose pushed open the door.

A rapier flashed. It whipped across a vase of flowers. One flower-head flew into the air and landed in the fencer's hand. The rapier itself sailed skywards. It spun twice before the fencer caught it neatly by the hilt.

Miss Regemont.

She turned and saw Rose.

'Ah!' she said, with a start. 'Miss Raventhorpe. I didn't hear you knock.'

'I – I didn't know you fenced,' stammered Rose.

Miss Regemont cleared her throat. She placed the rapier on her desk.

'Yes. Yes, I do. You wished to see me?'

Rose nodded and sat down.

'I assume you want to talk about poor Heddsworth,' the lady said. 'A travesty of justice! I have arranged for a London lawyer to defend him. Everything that can be done will be, I assure you.'

Rose swallowed. 'Actually I wanted to ask you about something else. Regarding Argyle.'

'Argyle?'

Rose felt her cheeks burn.

'I – I have just learned that – that you and he – had a romance. At one time.'

Miss Regemont stared at her.

'I beg your pardon?'

'I heard you had a romance,' Rose repeated.

'Did Argyle tell you this?'

'No!' said Rose. 'I – heard it elsewhere.'

Miss Regemont looked at the rapier on her desk.

'I'm sorry,' said Rose, bracing herself for Miss Regemont's anger. 'I didn't mean to upset you.'

'I'm not upset with you,' said Miss Regemont quietly. 'Just surprised. We kept it all so secret.'

'What?' gasped Rose. 'You mean it's true?'

The lady carried on, 'there was much you never knew about Argyle.'

Rose took the reprimand in guilty silence.

'We did have – an affection for each other,' said Miss Regemont.

Rose exhaled.

'But it ended?'

Miss Regemont's eyes flashed in sudden anger. 'It had to. You and your family were too important to him.'

'Me?' said Rose, taken aback. 'My family?'

'He was devoted to protecting you.' The words seemed to pour out of Miss Regemont. 'Ever since you were a baby. You came first. After Argyle's brother died, you were the only family he had. He longed to travel with your father. To see the Far East. But he knew you would be devastated if he left. We quarrelled over that. I got angry, and ended the relationship.'

'But he *was* going to go with Father,' whispered Rose. 'Before he died.'

'By then it was too late,' Miss Regemont snapped. 'He tried to find a suitable butler to go with your father – somebody trustworthy. Then the murders began, and there was no time to find anyone else. He had to go himself. But he never got his chance.'

Rose sat staring at her. She had never felt so

selfish and ashamed. Not even after her escapade in the Stairs Below. Her insides crumpled like burning paper. Had Argyle given up a dream, and adventure, to look after one indulged little girl? To teach her piano and tell her stories, as if he were a nurse or a governess?

Miss Regemont touched the rapier hilt. It bore an emblem of silver thistles.

'He gave me this blade,' she said softly.

He devoted his life to me, Rose thought. *And I gave nothing in return.*

'I was – devastated by his death. Believe me, Miss Raventhorpe, I want that killer found and brought to justice. But—' her voice faltered. 'I had to think of all the others I am responsible for.'

For a moment Rose found herself picturing Miss Regemont stabbing Argyle in a fit of anger. But no – that was like something out of Emily's Gothic poetry books. Miss Regemont had ended the romance, and mourned Argyle as a friend. She was hardly likely to go around stabbing butlers to death.

'But he must have been so unhappy,' Rose whispered. 'All that time he wanted to escape. He could have travelled. Had adventures. He . . . ' Her voice thickened. 'He wouldn't have died.'

Miss Regemont sighed. 'You can't be sure of that, Miss Raventhorpe.'

Rose wiped angrily at her eyes. 'But I wish he had gone to work for Father! I wouldn't have stopped him! Argyle could have buttled for Father, been his bodyguard . . . protected him. He could have gone abroad, it would have been a wonderful opportunity, the chance to work for a cause he believed in. His brother died from taking opium. Now some other butler will have to take his place, and . . . '

She stopped.

'Oh,' she breathed.

'What is it?' said Miss Regemont sharply.

Rose climbed slowly to her feet. She paced

around the room, muttering to herself. 'Yes . . . it could be . . . but if it was . . . oh, that does make sense! It's the motive.'

She turned back to Miss Regemont. 'The Black Glove murderer wasn't after an Infinity Key. He wanted to take Argyle's place.'

'What do you mean?' Miss Regemont demanded.

'Father asked Argyle to come and work for him in the Far East,' said Rose, still pacing back and forth. 'Father is an ambassador to the Crown, working to end the opium trade. What if someone wanted to stop him?'

'Well – I suppose – taking Argyle's place would be a good start,' mused Miss Regemont. 'But – oh! I see what you mean, Miss Raventhorpe. Argyle was murdered. If the murderer is a butler, he could take Argyle's job, and assassinate your father!'

'Exactly,' said Rose. She desperately needed to think clearly. 'Although the murderer could have killed Father when he was here. In Yorke. Why would someone go to the trouble of killing butlers, when he could have stabbed Father instead?'

'And why take the cat statues?' muttered Miss Regemont.

'Perhaps to make the murders look like a vendetta against all the butlers,' Rose suggested. 'As a means of misdirection. But if I'm right, there was a reason behind each murder. I think Guillaume and Tremayne wanted the job of going with Father to the Far East. They both asked you for references. Character references. You told us during the meeting at Silvercrest Hall. But when do most people need references? When they are applying for new positions!'

Miss Regemont stared at her. 'By Saint Iphigenia, Miss Raventhorpe . . . that would explain their deaths.'

'Working for my father would be more exciting and adventurous than working for a countess or a composer,' said Rose. 'Although it is strange – why didn't they tell you their plans?'

'I think I know,' sighed Miss Regemont. 'I helped both of them to get their situations in Yorke. It took some trouble. I suspect they felt badly about seeking a new place. So they did not tell me. But the Black Glove must have found out the truth. Perhaps they confided in him.'

'Someone they trusted,' agreed Rose.

'What about Herrick, Miss Raventhorpe? Why was he killed?' demanded Miss Regemont. 'Surely he didn't expect to take Argyle's place.'

'I think he was a witness to one of the murders,' mused Rose. 'Or the theft of the statues. The Black Glove killed him to keep him quiet.'

Miss Regemont nodded. 'Poor fellow. So, with Argyle dead, and a suitable time elapsed, the murderer writes to Lord Frederick to offer his services. You must confirm this with your father. Warn him, immediately.'

'I'll send him a telegram. I'll go straight home now and—'

Rose's voice trailed off.

'Miss Raventhorpe? What's the matter?'

'I – I've just remembered.' Rose had gone very pale. 'Mother is interviewing someone this afternoon. For the butler position. Miss Regemont – what if it's the murderer?'

Chapter 16

A Murderer Unmasked

Lady Constance was delighted. At last she had found a decent butler!

This applicant met every requirement – excellent references, experience and the right deferential demeanour. He even knew five different methods for cleaning chandeliers. The only defect was that he had been trained in Yorke, rather than London. *Well, in a backwater like the North one must put up with such things*, Her Ladyship reasoned.

One delicate issue remained. She gave a cough.

'You have heard, perhaps, of the fate of our late butler?'

The applicant inclined his head. 'A tragedy, madam. However, I assure you it will not keep me from my duties.'

Her Ladyship nodded. 'I am afraid my daughter had a childish attachment to him.'

'Her devotion does your daughter credit, madam,' said the butler courteously. 'But I am sure Your Ladyship will soon direct her interest to more . . . suitable friendships. If I may be so bold, the time will soon come for the Raventhorpe heiress to make a good marriage.'

Lady Constance smiled. 'I certainly hope so.'

'And may I say, madam, how happy I am at the prospect of serving Lord Frederick in the Far East. I would be most glad to travel abroad, and to assist His Lordship in fighting the opium trade. A worthy assignment in all respects.'

'You think so?' Lady Constance sighed. 'It

would be preferable if you stayed here, where I need a good butler. Still, it is not every man who would be willing to go far afield and serve his country as Lord Frederick does. I shall inform His Lordship.'

'Thank you, madam,' said the butler, bowing. 'I would consider it a great honour, indeed.'

'Miss Rose!' Agnes the maid nearly dropped her polishing-cloth. 'What's happened?'

'Where's Mother?' Rose gasped for breath, having run all the way from the Hall.

'Upstairs, miss.'

'Has she hired a new butler?'

'Aye, miss. Down the wine cellar, he is now.'

'Who is he? What's his name?'

'I haven't met him yet. Look here, miss, you'd better tidy up before Her Ladyship sees you.'

'I'm going to find the new butler first,' said Rose.

A bell rang. 'Oh dear,' said Agnes distractedly.

'Go on,' said Rose. 'I'll be all right.'

Agnes hesitated, but the bell rang again. With a last anxious look at Rose, she hurried away.

The steps down to the wine cellar were narrow and worn. Heart thumping, Rose descended. Lantern-light shone below. Wine bottles clinked.

She reached the last step.

The butler was somewhere in the depths of the cellar. It was big enough to contain hundreds of bottles of wine.

The air smelled of corks and oak barrels. Rose stepped quietly and carefully across the stone-flagged floor.

She could see his shadow now, cast by the lantern. He was walking slowly along the rows of racks, murmuring to himself, perhaps choosing bottles to serve at dinner.

When his shadow stopped moving, Rose stood as still as a cat statue. The butler paused. His shadow looked around. Not seeing anyone, he returned to his work.

Slowly, Rose crept up to him. She could see his back. It gave her a jolt of fury that Argyle's murderer was casually walking around Argyle's former domain.

She took another step.

The butler had been scrutinising labels. Now he turned in the lantern-light.

'Miss Raventhorpe!' he exclaimed.

Rose was stunned. There was a leaden-ball feeling in her stomach. Had she made a mistake? She must have. This couldn't be the murderer.

'Arundel?' she whispered.

In the lantern-light, he looked as he had at the cathedral. A dusty, ancient, vague sort of fellow, who was happiest reading old parchments. He didn't look strong enough to make a cup of tea, let alone wield a rapier.

'Dear me, Miss Raventhorpe,' he said. 'You did give me a start.'

'You're our new butler?' said Rose.

'Indeed I am.'

Rose struggled with her confusion. Why would Arundel want to hurt her father? Could it be that the Archbishop had ordered him to do it? But surely the Archbishop wouldn't do such a thing!

'Why are you here?' she stammered. 'You've left the Archbishop? You're going to work with Father?'

'It will sound silly to you,' said Arundel, wiping dust off a bottle. 'But ever since I was a boy, I have yearned to see faraway places. The exotic Orient! The spices of the Indies! For years I did my duty at the cathedral. But a dream is hard to let go of, Miss Raventhorpe. Now Argyle is gone, I feel it only right to care for your father in his place.'

Rose blinked in the dimness.

'You aren't afraid of the butler murderer?' she asked. 'The Black Glove? You said you were upset about the prophecy coming true.'

'Well, of course I am concerned,' said Arundel. 'Especially with Heddsworth in prison. But we must carry on. The Archbishop was very understanding about my decision, once I explained it all.'

Rose picked up a bottle Arundel had collected.

'This is one of Argyle's best Scotch whiskies,' she said. 'It's two hundred years old. He used to have it on his porridge.'

'Is it now?' Arundel peered at the label. 'Argyle gave you an interesting education!'

Rose gazed up at the dusty racks. Then at a nearby ladder.

'How did you get it down?'

'. . . I'm sorry?'

'You would have had to climb Argyle's ladder,' said Rose. 'The whiskies are kept on the top rack.'

'Ah yes,' said Arundel, sounding puzzled. 'Have I upset you by using it?'

'I just thought it strange,' said Rose. 'I mean, it

must have been quite a challenge for a man who couldn't climb the steps of Ladychurch Tower.'

She saw a flicker of something unpleasant in his eyes.

'I am not sure what you mean, Miss Raventhorpe.'

'When I was at the cathedral you said it wasn't easy for you to climb the steps to the Tower. Yet you are agile enough to climb a tall ladder.'

'I have better days than others,' said Arundel. He smiled, but there was a slight edge to his voice. 'And stairs are different to ladders. Now you must excuse me, Miss Raventhorpe. I have work to do.'

'How are you with a sword, Arundel?'

He picked up a silver corkscrew. 'Perhaps it is time you returned upstairs?'

Rose folded her arms.

'If you could climb a ladder, you could use one to take down the cat statues.'

'Miss Raventhorpe,' Arundel said coldly,

turning to face her. 'I know you are upset by the loss of Argyle, and by Heddsworth's current situation. But making wild accusations will not change unpleasant facts.'

'Were you watching me the day I talked to Herrick?' asked Rose, moving closer. 'Did you decide to get rid of him?'

'This is nonsense!'

'Why nonsense?'

'Miss Raventhorpe! I will not listen to this. You are a mere child, given to fancy. You give a beggar a pair of gloves, talk to him for a minute, and believe you can solve a crime? I am sorry to say this, but I will have to report your unladylike conduct to your mother.'

Rose looked him straight in the eye.

'How do you know,' she asked, 'that I gave Herrick a pair of gloves?'

There was a ringing silence.

'You . . . you told the butlers at Silvercrest Hall,' blustered Arundel.

'No I didn't.'

'Someone said it,' snapped Arundel. 'Heddsworth, I'm sure.'

'I'm going to warn my father about employing a murderer.'

'You will do no such thing!' Arundel suddenly flung out his arm. There was nothing vague about him now. He held the corkscrew like a rapier.

Rose stared at the corkscrew, only inches from her face. Arundel lowered his arm, his cold eyes fixed on Rose.

'You did it, didn't you?' said Rose. 'You murdered Argyle. And the others. All so you could take Argyle's place. Do you really want to kill my father?'

Arundel's features distorted with malice.

'Your father,' he said contemptuously, 'is a fool. He has money, privilege, power – all things he didn't work to get. I worked for years to establish myself in the opium trade!'

Rose gaped. 'You have an interest in that? You?'

Arundel snorted. 'Oh, I wouldn't, would I?' he mocked her. 'I'm only a mere, humble butler!'

'How—' Rose swallowed. 'How long have you been doing that?'

'Oh, if you want my whole life story – well, you are strangely interested in butlers. My father was an earl, Miss Raventhorpe. He threw out my mother – a mere servant – when she gave birth to me, so I was forced to work as a butler. Commonplace, servile work . . . but I was good at learning what my cloth-headed employers were up to. The Archbishop has useful contacts and friends, including your dear papa. I made investments in profitable trades. I used my brain, which I am happy to say is sharper than most. So I really do not appreciate your father's efforts to stop me.'

Rose's voice was thick with rage. 'So you were willing to kill people, people who trusted you, for the sake of business deals?'

'You are a pampered babe from the nursery,

Miss Raventhorpe. I don't hold with interference in my trade from His Lordship.'

'You murdered Argyle!'

'I saw no reason to hire assassins when I could do the job myself,' said Arundel, with a shrug. 'Tremayne and Guillaume told me they were considering going overseas with your father. So they had to go. It was simple to make it look like an attack on all the Hall's butlers.'

'That's why you took down the cat statues.'

'Surprisingly easy,' said Arundel. 'I went disguised as a lamplighter. And it was amusing to see how much it upset everyone.'

'I knew there had to be a connection,' said Rose.

Arundel looked her up and down.

'I suspected you might work it out,' he said slowly, 'ever since you started asking those questions in the drapers'.'

'I thought the Crows were responsible at first,' Rose admitted. 'Or Dr Jankers. You were clever.'

He gave her a thin-lipped smile. 'The Crows have their uses. As do the Stairs Below.'

'And Heddsworth,' snapped Rose. 'Accused of committing your crimes.'

'He may not hang,' said Arundel. 'But if he does – well, sometimes one must sacrifice a worthy opponent.'

'You're a common murderer. I'm surprised you didn't kill Father when he was here, in Yorke!'

'I could have.' Arundel's eyes were icy. 'But I would have no access to his letters, or his records or contacts. If I went abroad with him as his butler, I could learn so much useful information. I can get rid of Lord Frederick in the Far East when it suits me. When he is no longer worth keeping alive.'

'You won't go anywhere near my father!'

'Oh, I disagree,' said Arundel softly. 'I am in your household now. I am sure you want your mother and servants to be safe. Do you understand, Miss Raventhorpe? I have suggested to your mother that you need better supervision. A strict governess, perhaps . . . or school abroad. I dare say she is making arrangements as we speak.'

'It's more likely,' said another voice, 'that she'll be telling His Lordship to kick your backside.'

Charlie Malone stood in the doorway. His pistol was aimed at Arundel.

Chapter 17

Return of the Guardians

'Miss Regemont told me to follow you, Miss Raventhorpe,' said Charlie Malone. 'You left in something of a hurry.'

Rose felt a mixture of elation and fear. Did Charlie realise how dangerous Arundel must be?

'You're a coward, Arundel,' Charlie said softly. 'The Black Glove, the terror of Yorke. Threatening a child. Stabbing unarmed men. I'm surprised you didn't stab them in the back. That wouldn't bother the likes of you.'

Arundel's astonishment turned to a sneer. 'Ah, the Hall's resident cripple! Playing bodyguard to Miss Raventhorpe now?'

'I'm putting you out of action,' snarled Charlie. 'Keep your hands where I can see them. Rose, would you lead the way upstairs?'

To Rose's astonishment, Arundel lowered his hands.

'I don't think you'll fire that weapon in a wine cellar,' he told Charlie Malone, with a smirk. 'Too much risk of a ricochet. We don't want a bullet to strike the wrong person, do we?'

He threw the corkscrew at Charlie. The young man ducked, and Arundel rushed for the stairs.

Rose and Charlie rushed after him. They ran to the front door and then outside, into the foggy street. Rose picked up her skirts and ran after Arundel. She was faster than Charlie, and if she could delay Arundel long enough for Charlie to catch up—

Someone shoved violently into her, sending her

sprawling on the cobblestones. She heard cries and thuds. Dazed, she struggled up on her hands and knees.

Arundel stood over Charlie, holding his pistol.

'Now then, Mr Malone,' purred Arundel. 'You don't want that other leg damaged. After all, I was responsible for the first one.'

Charlie threw himself upwards and lashed out at Arundel. Arundel slammed the pistol down on Charlie's temple. The young man collapsed like a puppet.

'Now, Miss Raventhorpe,' said Arundel, pointing the pistol at her. 'Should I silence you? You should have heeded my warnings. I tried to scare you off by throwing that dead cat at you.'

Rose was bracing herself for the sting of a bullet when she heard footsteps.

Two figures emerged from the fog. One was Bronson, rapier drawn. The other – to Rose's joy – was Heddsworth. He carried a pistol, and wore a rapier under his coat.

'Drop it, Arundel,' said Heddsworth. 'Now.'

Arundel hesitated.

'I think we know which one of us is the better shot,' said Heddsworth. 'If you dare harm Miss Raventhorpe, you won't live another second.'

Rage contorted Arundel's face. Then he bolted into the shadows.

Bronson knelt to attend Charlie.

'Bruises, cracked ribs, a probable concussion . . . can you move your hands, Charlie? Your legs?'

Charlie struggled into sitting position. 'It's not as bad as it looks,' he gasped. 'Miss Raventhorpe?'

'I'm all right,' said Rose, shaking uncontrollably.

'Heddsworth, give her some brandy,' Bronson ordered. 'There's some in my coat pocket.'

Heddsworth extracted the bottle. 'What about Mr Malone?'

'Don't bother about me,' spluttered Charlie. 'Go after Arundel!'

'I'll find him.' Bronson leapt to her feet, hand on her rapier hilt. 'That poxing, festering, rotting traitor – I'll run him through for this!'

Rose coughed as the brandy seared her throat. She gave the bottle gladly back to Heddsworth. 'Heddsworth – how did you get out of prison?'

'We had some help from Dr Jankers,' said Heddsworth.

'Dr Jankers?' cried Rose in amazement.

'He was keen to help us after we proved young Mortloyd was a Crow. Bronson got him to visit the prison, on the pretext of asking about bodies for his medical work. Then he offered the guard a drink of brandy drugged with Necrodrops. Once he was snoring, Bronson pilfered his keys.'

'We can chat later,' snapped Charlie, now wavering on his feet. 'Bronson and Heddsworth, you go look for Arundel around the Shudders. Rose and I will walk towards the cathedral.'

'I'll take Charlie to the cathedral. That will be safe,' Rose insisted. 'You have to catch Arundel.'

Bronson and Heddsworth exchanged glances.

'The Shudders, then,' said Heddsworth at last.

'Here, Mr Malone, Bronson brought a spare.' He gave Charlie a rapier. Then he cocked his pistol. Bronson lifted her blade, and they disappeared down the skitterway.

Charlie leaned heavily against a wall. Rose took his arm.

'Come along. The cathedral's not far off.'

Reluctantly Charlie put a hand on her shoulder. He took a step. Rose's knees shook, but she went resolutely forward.

The fog was even thicker now, and the cold was piercing. Rose had to clench her teeth to stop them from chattering.

The expanse of lawn circling Yorke Cathedral had never seemed so wide. But it was a welcome sight after the dark, narrow streets. The cathedral glowed before them, lighted with candles. They struggled up the steps and through the doorway.

The great nave smelled of candle-wax. Charlie dropped gratefully into a pew. Despite the cold, his face was damp with sweat.

'I'll get you some water,' said Rose.

Charlie tried to smile. Then he closed his eyes, breathing shallowly.

Rose hurried through the nave. A movement caught her eye.

Watchful the cat. By Arlington's tomb. He lashed his tail angrily, blinking uncanny golden eyes. Rose stared. Then she gasped. The tomb's lid had been pushed aside.

She braced herself, walked up to the tomb, and looked inside.

No shrouded corpse. No bones. Just a tangle of ironwork. What on earth were those things? The curl of a tail . . . an ear . . .

Rose gripped the edge of the tomb. She had found the stolen cat statues of Yorke!

'Missed them, have you?' said a voice.

Arundel emerged from the door of Ladychurch Tower.

'For pity's sake,' he spat. 'I come back here to hide and you're here? Can I not get rid of you?'

He held a rapier now, as well as Charlie's pistol.

'You hid the statues in the tomb,' said Rose numbly.

'The prophecy of the statues,' he mocked. 'How easily it scares people. The statues have disappeared! The city is doomed!'

Rose eyed the rapier. How had he got that? And how had he got here?

'The Stairs Below,' she said. 'You have a hidden door here?'

'Correct again,' Arundel said. 'Quite the detective, Miss Raventhorpe.' He jabbed the pistol at her. 'Get in that tomb.'

For a moment Rose didn't understand. Then she went numb with shock. He was going to shut her in the tomb with the statues.

'Hurry up,' snapped Arundel.

Suddenly he yelped. Watchful had sunk his claws into his leg. Arundel swore, kicking the animal aside. 'You disgusting, flea-ridden feline!'

He fired a shot, which pinged off one of the cat

statues. Then he lowered his pistol and aimed it at Rose.

Rose caught her breath. The expected shot did not come. To her astonishment Arundel gazed into space, his eyes wide and terrified.

'Get them away from me!'

Rose could see nothing. She stayed frozen in place as he staggered backwards, swiping at the air.

'That's not possible,' he whispered.

Rose stared. Watchful sat crouched and hissing, five feet away. Then she saw *it*. The statues in the tomb were . . . changing.

Cloudy cat-shapes, with fiery eyes, circling and hissing and switching their tails . . . slashing with their claws . . . nipping with sharp teeth. Rents appeared in Arundel's clothing.

'Get them off me!'

The ghostly figures circled Arundel, forcing him backwards. One of the creatures paced around Watchful, who suddenly turned into a smoky effigy himself. Rose gasped.

They were closing in on Arundel. He came to the edge of the stairway. The cats hissed again.

Arundel lashed out at them with his rapier, to no effect.

The cats leapt at him, and he fell. Down the secret stairway. Down to the Stairs Below.

Footsteps sounded behind her. Rose turned to see Charlie Malone. White-faced, bloodstained, swaying, borrowed rapier in hand. He frowned.

'Rose – was that Arundel?'

She opened her mouth to explain.

An ominous rumbling came from the ground beneath their feet.

Rose felt a moment's puzzlement. It sounded like thunder, but not quite. The floor was vibrating. It was as if the cathedral itself was growling in rage.

Charlie grabbed Rose's hand and pulled her under an archway. Watchful dashed away like black lightning.

There was a deafening crash.

Rose stared at the walls in horror. The prophecy flashed into her mind:

But if the cats are taken
Then the Guardians will fall
The dead will rise up from their graves
And ruin will come to all.

Paving-stones fractured. Clouds of thick dust billowed from cracks. Rose and Charlie coughed. The roar subsided to a tumbling clatter of stones.

The cathedral still stood.

The space beyond the door was filled with fallen rock. Arundel's secret tunnel to the Stairs Below had caved in, burying him in rubble.

Watchful the cat strolled past, looking completely solid and normal again. Rose reached out a tremulous hand to touch him. Had she really seen him change?

She looked at the silent room. The cat statues

of Yorke were back in the tomb, mere statues again. Dust settled around the words carved on Arlington's tomb: *Traitors will imprisoned be beneath a wall of stone.* The tomb, Rose saw, had not even cracked.

Chapter 18

The New Butler

Lady Constance sighed over her breakfast kippers.

'Really, it is too bad about Arundel. Gone without a word of notice! One simply cannot find the staff these days.'

'Yes, terrible,' said Rose, trying to keep her face straight.

She turned the pages of the newspaper. An article said that a suspect in the Butler Murders had been released from prison. The real Black Glove was presumed dead. Police had taken statements from certain persons of interest (Miss Regemont and Lord Frederick, following a flurry of telegrams), and some property belonging to the city had been recovered. Meanwhile, the Archbishop of Yorke was looking for a new butler.

There was a knock at the front door. Agnes answered it, and came back to say, 'Miss Proops and a young man, madam.'

'A young man?' Rose stared at Agnes.

Lady Constance sighed. 'Oh, very well. Invite them into the parlour, Agnes. I should write to Emily's mother. Her standards are slipping atrociously.'

Rose flew to the parlour. Emily appeared, in her best black dress, holding hands with—

Harry Dodge.

'Hello, Rose,' said Emily, blushing deepest pink. 'I'd like to introduce you to my fiancé, Mr Harry Dodge.'

*

Agnes brought tea and Yorke buns. The guests sat together on the sofa, cooing to each other.

'It was love at first sight, wasn't it, Harry darling?'

'From the moment you flung back that mourning veil I was smitten,' Dodge declared. 'We are twin souls. United by the universe.'

'You were the master of my heart,' breathed Emily, 'from the moment you appeared onstage. I felt the call of Fate. Of all the people in that theatre, you spoke to me alone.'

'Goddess of the Netherworld!' Dodge kissed her fingertips. 'My jet-clad beauty.'

Emily turned to the flabbergasted Rose. 'You must be my bridesmaid, Rose darling!'

'I – I'd be delighted,' said Rose. 'I just can't believe I didn't know you were in love!'

'Well, we had to keep it quiet at first,' said Dodge. 'Which was very exciting, wasn't it dearest?'

'Oh it was,' sighed Emily. 'A forbidden love! We had to send notes in secret.'

'Spillwell took them for us,' explained Dodge. 'I think the old fellow's a secret romantic. Went by the Stairs Below, even though he wasn't supposed to.'

Rose felt her jaw drop. She had suspected Spillwell of murder, when he had been carrying love letters!

'He said it was a matter of family honour to keep it secret,' said Emily, giggling. 'But I have caught him reading romance novels on the sly.'

'So your parents have agreed to the marriage, Emily?' Rose asked.

'Oh, it took a while,' said Emily. 'I'm still awfully young, you know. And darling Harry's life on the stage isn't quite what Mama and Papa wanted for me. But we talked them into it. Papa said "at least we shall hear less of the blasted poetry". Isn't he a funny old thing?'

'I'm so glad for you!' said Rose.

'And Harry has given me a new Pomeranian dog. I have named him Bertram the Second.

We will take him hot-air ballooning for our honeymoon.'

When the happy couple had gone, Rose told the news to her mother. Lady Constance sniffed. 'Miss Proops to wed a mere entertainer! Well, this is what comes of living so far from London.'

Agnes reappeared, and curtsied. 'M'lady? The new butler is in the drawing-room for his interview.'

Rose started. 'The new what?'

'I have found a new butler,' replied her mother. 'Someone,' she added witheringly, 'who will be mindful of his place. You may come with me, Rose. You must learn how these things are done.'

Reluctantly, Rose followed her.

Her Ladyship sat down on the sofa. Rose perched on a chair. The new applicant bowed.

When Rose saw his face, she had a sudden fit of coughing.

'Now,' said Lady Constance, flicking through

papers. 'Your references seem all in order. Perhaps you could tell us more about your previous placings.'

'Certainly, madam. I have worked for the Sheikh of Gazal, who was most happy with my service. Then there was Lady McBeath of London. I also served Sir Richard Cliptree of Uffington Park. All were excellent employers. Now, I would consider it an honour to serve the Raventhorpe household. I am aware of previous sadness,' he added, with a glance at Rose. 'I cannot replace an old friend, but I will do my best to live up to his standards.'

Lady Constance consulted the references again. 'Very well. Shall we say a trial period of two weeks?'

'Thank you, madam. I am most obliged.'

Lady Constance prepared to vacate the sofa.

'One last matter, madam,' said the butler respectfully. 'Would a pet be permitted in your establishment?'

Lady Constance was taken aback. 'A pet? What kind of pet?'

The butler took a wicker basket from behind a chair. He drew out a furry black creature. Rose put a hand to her mouth.

'A cat?' Lady Constance recoiled.

'Oh, this is a feline of pedigree, madam.'

Lady Constance still looked uncertain.

Rose spoke up. 'I think it's a good idea, Mother. Mrs Standish would appreciate a cat in the kitchen.'

'Hmm – well – the creature may remain, then. You must be responsible for him, Mr—' she consulted a reference. 'Heddsworth.'

'You are very kind, madam.'

'I leave you to your duties.' Lady Constance rose to her feet. 'You must excuse me, I am going out to pay some calls. Rose, remember your piano practice.'

She swept out the front door, where her carriage waited.

Rose whirled around, a huge smile on her face. 'Heddsworth! You might have told me!'

'And spoil the surprise?' Heddsworth looked as dignified as ever, but his eyes gleamed with mischief.

'And Watchful!' Rose bent to pet him. 'The Archbishop gave him to you?'

'Indeed he did. Of course, the final choice lies with Watchful. There is no keeping a cat where he does not want to stay.'

Rose swallowed. The events in the cathedral, where she had seen Watchful and the other ghostlike cats, seemed hard to believe in the light of day. Dare she tell Heddsworth about it?

'He's a proper Guardian,' she said at last.

'Yes,' said Heddsworth. 'I know.'

'Heddsworth . . . about Father. He's not truly safe now, is he? There will be others wanting to assassinate him.'

'I fear so, Miss Raventhorpe.'

'Well . . . if you want to work for him – if you

want to travel – that's all right. I mean, it's far more important that he is protected than me.'

Heddsworth's eyes crinkled.

'I am honoured by your trust, Miss Raventhorpe. But I am sure we could find another suitable butler for His Lordship. I know a few potential candidates already.'

'You do?' Rose couldn't help smiling.

'Oh yes. Now, would you oblige me, Miss Raventhorpe, by showing me to the kitchen? Before I start my duties, I think we could both do with a nice cup of tea.'

Yorke's graveyard was tranquil at dusk. Mist rose from the ground in a silvery veil. When the iron gate creaked open, it barely disturbed a living creature. Four people and a cat walked down the path.

At the sight of some birds, the cat took on a predatory gait. 'Don't even think of it,' warned Rose.

They went to the foot of Argyle's grave.

Heddsworth crouched down and dug a hole with a trowel. Charlie Malone held out a potted briar rose.

The others stood respectfully by as Rose set the plant in place, and patted down the earth. In spring, its scarlet blossoms would climb over the mortsafe.

'I brought these,' said Bronson, proffering a pot of marigolds. 'Argyle always liked yellow.'

'They're lovely,' said Rose. 'We'll put them around the edges.'

There was another floral tribute under the mortsafe – a posy of roses and thistles. Rose had a good idea of who had left them there. Miss Regemont would have made her visit alone, in private.

Charlie took a flask from his coat pocket, and a couple of goblets. He poured a libation of whisky into each vessel and handed them around to the butlers. Rose was given a cup of Scottish spring water.

'To Argyle,' Heddsworth said, and they drank. Heddsworth sprinkled a few drops over the mortsafe. Watchful squeezed through the bars and curled up comfortably on the grave.

Bronson glanced around.

'The Crows wouldn't dare show their faces now,' she said, with satisfaction. 'The Lord Mayor is finally increasing the penalties for grave-robbery.'

'Best to be ready, just in case,' Charlie pointed out.

'Yes, we shall be. Now, you must excuse Miss Raventhorpe and me,' Heddsworth told the others. 'We have pressing matters to attend to. Bronson, if you would be so kind, take Watchful back to Miss Raventhorpe's house.'

Bronson's brows lifted indignantly. 'Pressing matters? What could be so pressing? Wait – Charlie, that's not how you space marigolds. Did no one teach you gardening? Here, you lay them out like this—'

Heddsworth and Rose began to walk towards the cathedral.

'Now,' said Heddsworth. 'Where shall we start? I rather think Ravensgate.'

'Oh yes,' said Rose. 'And then Vicarsgate, and up near the Clarion . . . '

Heddsworth chuckled. 'Don't be too ambitious, Miss Raventhorpe! This will be a tricky operation. We will have to access each building, possibly climb roofs . . . '

'I know the prophecy,' declared Rose. 'I'm taking no chances.'

Smiling, Heddsworth nodded at Rose's cameo. 'Very well. What say we take the Stairs Below?'

Rose beamed back.

They used Rose's Infinity Key to open the door to the Stairs. Then they walked by lantern-light all the way to Silvercrest Hall.

Heddsworth brought a horse and wagon from the stables. Rose climbed in, and pulled a moth-eaten dress over her own. She put on a comfortable dark jacket, then a hat so she could tuck up her hair, and laced on a pair of boots.

They drove first to Ravensgate. The stars were out, and the street quiet. Heddsworth took a ladder from the cart and placed it securely at the foot of a building.

Rose lifted the Ravensgate cat statue from its wrappings. It was heavy, but she held on to it tightly. Heddsworth steadied the ladder as Rose carefully climbed up. She reached the deep ledge where the cat usually sat, and set the statue securely in its place. The cat looked vigilant, gazing over the city streets.

'All done?' called Heddsworth. 'My turn next. We have plenty more to go.'

'We'll manage it,' said Rose, and climbed swiftly back down the ladder. By morning, the cat statues of Yorke would be back where they belonged.

All the same, Rose had a feeling they would

have a lot to watch out for in the coming months. She knew the butlers would be ready. *And so will I*, she thought exultantly, closing her fingers around her cameo. *So will I.*

Letters from a Hot-Air Balloon

Dear Rose,

We seem to have drifted off course, but it is very pleasant in the Hebrides. I am knitting a vest for Bertram the Second.

Scotland is most atmospheric. Majestic deer, and darling hairy cows. Bertram adores them. He races around in circles, while the 'coos' regard him with typical Scottish aplomb.

Your airborne friend,

Emily Dodge (Mrs)

PS. Thank you, dear Rose, for being my bridesmaid. You looked wonderful in that hat from Madcaps and Ribbons. I thought the pink lovebirds were the perfect touch.

Dear Rose,

Here we are in Cornwall. We landed in a field near Tintagel, and cooked our breakfast in the castle ruins. Harry said he could hear the spirits of the medieval past, crying out in battle. However, that turned out to be Bertram, stealing the sausages out of the pan. His whiskers were only mildly singed.

Your dear friend,

Emily P. Dodge

Dear Rose,

We have landed the balloon on the Yorkesborough moor, so we could visit our favourite author, Miss Jane Wildcliffe. She has a fierce dog and a tame eagle. We offered her a balloon-ride, but she said she prefers communing with nature at ground level. She seemed a bit cross that we had found her refuge (a most picturesque and primitive ruined castle). However, we managed to get her to sign our copies of her books. I am saving one for you.

With fondest affection,

Emily D.

Dear Rose,

I am not entirely sure how we ended up in Jersey. Harry says it is his own fault, as the map blew overboard. Bertram has chewed up our compass. We are navigating by the stars and the sun, which is most romantic. Though rather difficult on a cloudy day.

Your travelling friend,

Emily (Mrs Harry Dodge)

Dear Rose,

Tell Spillwell and Heddsworth it was very kind of them to bring Papa's carriage all the way to Wales to rescue us. They even had flasks of hot tea, and scones!

I am sure your father would adore hot-air ballooning. Next summer we shall all go, with you and your butler friends!

Must go. Spillwell is getting very tetchy about holding Bertram the Second.

All my love,

Emily

Glossary

A List of Odd Words and Fun Facts

Tear-catcher bottle: Victorians loved making a show of their grief. A tear-catcher was a small bottle you wore around your neck, or carried with you. When you cried for your lost loved one, you caught the tears in the bottle. After a year you were meant to pour the tears on to the grave of the departed one. You could get almost anything in black for mourning, including hairpins and tiaras.

Skitterways: I called the little alleyways and snickets in the city of Yorke 'skitterways'. I hope this sounds like the skittering of alley cats, ducking from place to place. A twentieth-century author gave the alleys in York, UK the wonderful name of Snickelways. Sadly for me, this name didn't exist in the Victorian era.

The Shudders: The Shudders is based on the Shambles, a picturesque, ancient street in the real York. It was once full of butchers' shops. Now it is a popular tourist attraction.

Bodysnatchers: People needed to install mortsafes over graves when bodysnatching became a way to make money. Doctors would pay the bodysnatchers, also called resurrectionists, for fresh corpses to dissect. In the famous Burke and Hare case, two men turned to murder to provide the corpses. Public outrage led to new laws, and when doctors could legally access the bodies of executed criminals, the practice of bodysnatching faded out in the 1840s. In my imaginary Yorke, it goes on for quite a while afterwards.

Cat statues: There really are cat statues on buildings in York. Most have been put up quite recently, but they were inspired by much older versions. Legend has it they were meant to scare off vermin from the city.

Streets: York has many '-gate' street names, dating from Viking times ('gata' was Viking for 'street'). I have made up my own names for this book.

Duels: Pistol and sword duels were common in the Victorian and Edwardian eras. One famous duel between a princess and a countess took place in 1892. It was over a flower arrangement.

Acknowledgements

My thanks go to Polly Nolan and Sarah Davies, the amazing agents who took a chance on me. Also to Karen Ball, who fell in love with Rose's world (I still wish I'd been at that meeting!), Katherine Agar and Becca Allen, editors extraordinaire. You are openers of doors, lights in the labyrinth, and my own personal Infinity Keys.